JOURNEY TO FOREVER
BOOK II

GATEWAY TO THE WILDERNESS

JOURNEY TO FOREVER
BOOK II
GATEWAY TO THE WILDERNESS

RONALD M. ROBINSON

aventine press

Published by Aventine Press
55 East Emerson St.
Chula Vista CA 91911
www.aventinepress.com

ISBN: 978-1-955162-06-7

Library of Congress Control Number: 2021923874
Library of Congress Cataloging-in-Publication Data
Ronald M. Robinson/Gateway to the Wilderness

Printed in the United States of America

Table of Contents

Characters

The Barbarians
Stat (chieftain)
Rakker (chieftain's cousin)
Letog (member of chieftain's council)

Dogwood
Baron Durkel (Baron of Dogwood)
Franklin (scribe under the baron)
Quayfear (scribe under the baron)
Baker (Knight of Dogwood)

Driftwood
Puah (slave)

Edgewood
Montague {commander of Edgewood)
Brom (Knight of Edgewood)
Hadrian (Knight of Edgewood)
Oliver (Knight of Edgewood)
(one more unnamed knight of Edgewood)

Fartherwood
Harbinger
Kingsley (Harbinger's best friend)
Luther (woodworker)
Driscoll (tavern manager)
John (worked at tavern)
Brandish (Daria's brother)
Lady Kettery (of the Kettery manor)
Daria (servant of the manor)
Beth (servant of the manor)
Ursula (servant of the manor)

Genadar
prince of Genadar
(all servants of the prince)
Banebreath
Blackrose
Brainwart
Marshstench
Number Two
Sandgrit
Sourlip
Stumprot

Seven
Charles (tavern proprietor)

The Great City
Page (the emissary)
Merrill (commander under the emissary)
Ewar (palace guard)
Gavin (palace guard)
Kai (palace guard)
Peyton (palace guard)
Thomas (palace guard)
Tobias (palace guard)
Tybalt (palace guard)
(two more unnamed palace guards)

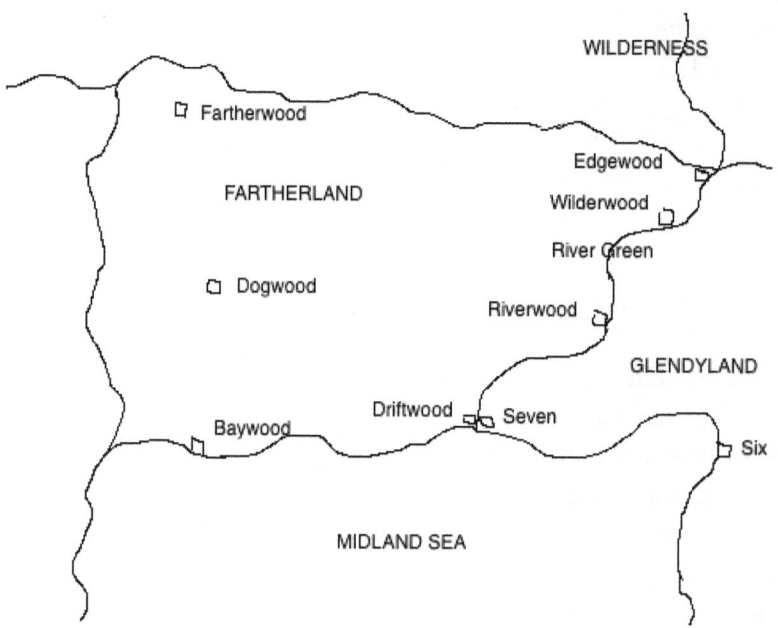

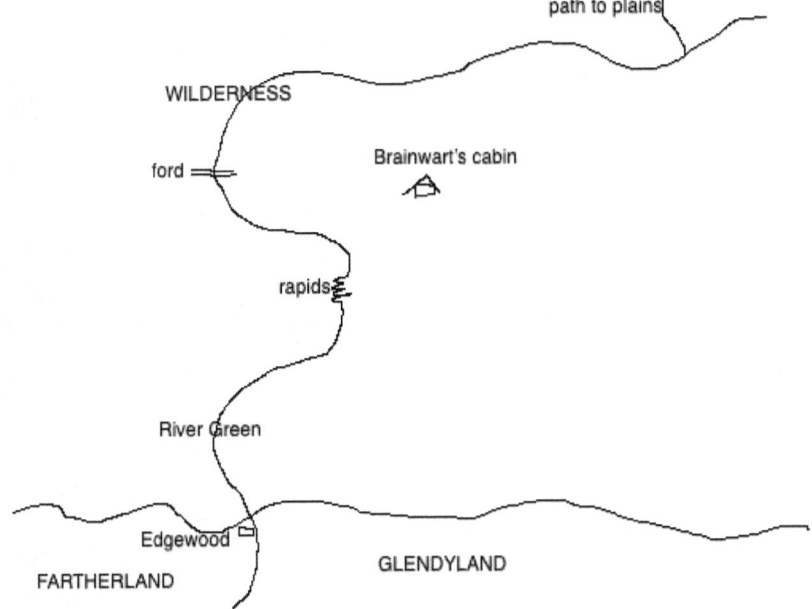

"Nevertheless my eye spared them from destruction. I did not make an end of them in the wilderness."

Ezekiel 20:17 [NKJV]

Prologue, the first: Leaving Fartherwood

It began when Brandish's mother received word from the prophet Dresler that her son would play a major role in defeating an evil lord. But it isn't until eighteen years later, when Brandish shows up at a tavern in Fartherwood planning to begin a new life as a blacksmith journeyman that the adventure truly begins. Brandish is intent on leaving the next day for his new life in The Great City ...which he does, but not before hearing of a mysterious scroll found behind the tavern.

That spring eve in the tavern, Brandish and seven others hear the contents of that scroll. It instructs those assembled to travel through the wilderness to assist a White King in a great battle in the city of Vale to be waged by midsummer. Franklin and Quayfear (scribes under Baron Durkel of Dogwood), Luther (a woodworker), Driscoll and John (who works at the tavern), and Kingsley and Harbinger (young men hoping to become knights of the Midland Realm) venture into the wilderness per the scroll's orders the next day. Franklin leads the others on this quest, though only Franklin truly believes its prophecy.

At that same time, the Baron Durkel is ordered by a demonic power sent by the Prince of Genadar to find that scroll - which he fails to do. So the Baron, with a few of his men, leaves Fartherwood in pursuit of those who have found it.

When the Baron disappears and his men are discovered brutally murdered, Page, the emissary of King Fenelon, and eleven palace guards are tasked to give chase to the motley crew with the scroll.

After a couple of days, only Franklin and John (a boy of fourteen) continue the implausible quest. Harbinger, Kingsley, Driscoll, Quayfear, and Luther return to Fartherwood to discover they are unjustifiably sought for the brutal deaths of the Baron's men.

Driscoll is caught first and assists the king's emissary as a spy to seek information from Harbinger's fiancé as to the whereabouts of the others.

Kingsley turns himself in to the emissary in hope for leniency.

Harbinger and Quayfear ride out of the hamlet only to later be captured by some of the palace guards sent to find them.

Franklin and John, who still follow the scroll, opt for travel along the River Green, and bump into Luther who successfully escaped Fartherwood.

Brandish finally believes that the prophet, the one his mother had insisted since his childhood called him to greatness as a leader, is in Fartherwood. But by the time he returns, the prophet has gone and the adventurers dispersed. Discovering that Franklin, a simple scribe, leads the group, Brandish is angry and disillusioned until convinced that when the time is right he will inherit his rightful place as leader.

Yet all looks hopeless for fulfillment of any prophecy: the adventurers are scattered, some aiding the emissary, others captured, and the rest facing demons sent by the dark Prince.

As for the Baron, by then he has sided with the Prince of Genadar and has begun recruiting the barbarians for the Prince's evil goals. The first objective: The city of Vale which could then open the entire western border of the Midland Realm to the Prince's evil minions.

Beth Makes a Move

Brandish sat staring at the closed door after the prophet's assistant Sourlip departed from the room on the second floor of The Shady Inn in Wilderwood. Brandish was flustered, drained, and exhausted as if he had just run up a bare hill against a stinging horizontal rain while rampant wolves followed close behind. As time slowly and painstakingly elapsed the feeling of perturbation began to dissipate and a sense of normalcy returned to his room. The air was lighter, the brooding aura relieved.

Brandish could think clearly again. The news that Sourlip had brought forth that he would have to find Franklin in Wilderwood and assist him was disturbing yet hopeful. He would begin his search in the morning.

*

Brandish awoke to voices coming from outside the inn. He opened the wooden shutters over the small square window and glanced up Tenth Street. He was surprised to see the palace guard but even more astounded to see Harbinger, Kingsley, and Franklin's friend Quayfear from Dogwood with them.

He recalled that Beth had mentioned some of the Baron's knights were killed and that Harbinger and Kingsley would most likely bear the brunt of the blame. *They've been caught.* Brandish pulled his head back into the room when he saw them nearing the inn. He squatted below his window to listen. The horses came to a halt. He heard one of the men enter the inn.

"Well," said Ewar to his party upon exiting the rundown establishment, "the journeyman guild is on Third Street."

"And Kingsley," Merrill added, "you can recognize Luther?"

"I know him well."

"If he's there, that makes three. Ewar and Tybalt, tomorrow you will escort our prisoners to Edgewood, our fortress along the northern border of the wilderness."

Brandish heard the movement of horses and the men's voices fading. *It seems that Kingsley in exchange for leniency has turned himself in to identify the others, and Luther is next.* Brandish quickly got dressed. Luther was of no concern, but it was imperative he find Franklin before they did.

*

Merrill knocked on the door of the journeyman guild on Third Street. An older man answered of jovial countenance. When he saw the regalia of the palace guard, he quickly took on a more somber poise, and said, "My lord, please come in." Merrill and two knights entered.

The several young guildsmen stopped what they were doing and wondered at what had brought the palace guard from The Great City to their doorstep. The young wood wrights had spoken often amongst themselves of such adventures to far-flung parts of the Realm, the admiration they would receive wherever they went and the endless attention of lust filled damsels. Likewise the two knights took note of the pleasant fragrance of curled cedar shavings on the floor which permeated the air, the peaceful camaraderie and warm dry atmosphere as opposed to endless travel in inclement weather, and marveled at the normalcy of such a life.

"What is it my lord?" the instructor asked the emissary's underling.

"We are looking for a man named Luther scheduled to arrive here from an apprentice guild in Fartherwood. Is he here?"

"No, my lord, I do not expect my apprentice from Fartherwood till the next full moon."

"Being an exceptional woodworker he was dispatched early," Merrill contrived. "However, he is wanted for questioning by the emissary."

"In trouble he is?"

"Possibly - if he arrives, assign him duties as usual. Meanwhile send me word of his arrival. I will be staying at the River's Inn."

"Yes, my lord, and you said his name is Luther. I can assure you that I will make contact with you when he arrives."

"Your loyalty will not go unrewarded," Merrill said assuredly and departed.

*

Lady Kettery along with Ursula, Driscoll, and Blackrose had been traveling south from Fartherwood in hopes of catching up with the emissary. They arrived in Dogwood about midday. "Woe," said Ursula as she pulled back on the reins. The wagon came to a halt in front of the large castle.

Ursula tilted her head back, mouth opened wide as she gazed up at the high stone fortress. Lady Kettery rolled her eyes at the simpleton's dumbfounded reaction to life outside of their rural community and turned toward the two sitting behind her. Driscoll was rubbing his stiff aching legs, and the dutiful Blackrose sat attentively, simply there to respond to any command from her mistress. "You two wait here," Lady Kettery said to them. "Ursula, come with me."

The blonde servant followed her mistress up the broad stairway to the main door snapping her head back towards the others with a snide superior look on her face. Driscoll was not angered or aroused by it. He glanced over at Blackrose unique in her perspective, subservient yet disconnected to it all.

Lady Kettery now wondered if the Duchess would actually remember her. They were twenty years apart in age, and it had been a long time since they had seen each other.

Lady Kettery stopped before a knight who stood by the front entrance, and said without hesitation as if the knight might know her from some past life, "My good sir, would you please inform the Duchess that Lady Kettery from Fartherwood is here." The man immediately went inside assuming that this woman was expected by the Duchess. Lady Kettery glanced up at her tall servant who was genuinely impressed with her mistress.

She and Ursula noticed the Duchess approach the bright entrance from the dingy shadows of the dark interior with a degree of expectation. Lady Kettery was impressed how this mature woman now carried herself so poised and refined, hardly the little girl she remembered long ago. Lady Kettery breathed a sigh of relief as she saw a warm smile greet her – *she remembers*.

"Why, Lady Kettery!" The excited Duchess proclaimed. "What has brought you here?" Though wanting to give her a hug, she refrained, remembering how stiff and formal she was and from the looks of things that hadn't changed.

Lady Kettery began, "Much has happened in our small hamlet of late. I'm sure you have heard it so from the emissary who must have just passed through - if he isn't still here," she added hopefully.

"No, my lady, he is not here. He left yesterday morning."

"Mm," she murmured, "then we can't stay long, but we could use a decent meal and a chance to clean up a little."

"Of course, my lady," she said and turned to the guard. "Fetch some servants to tend to our guests and tell Broso to prepare a quick meal." She smiled at Lady Kettery. "Come, while we wait, we can talk."

At that moment two of the Duchess' servants went by in a flurry down the stone stairway toward the buck port. The Duchess led Lady Kettery through the grand foyer of the castle and along a straight corridor which led to a door which opened onto a courtyard. Two gardeners were busy cleaning the area. "Why don't you men take a rest from your labor," said the Duchess. "I need to talk to Lady Kettery from Fartherwood…alone."

After the men left, the Duchess pointed to two cedar chairs at the extreme end of the courtyard. The air was raw. A bank of clouds had rolled in since the morning. Lady Kettery would rather have been sitting in a comfortable study by a warm hearth but understood the Duchess needed a place they could talk without any chance of being overheard.

"May I speak frankly my lady?" the Duchess said.

"I should think so since that is why you have me sit out here in this dank weather. This thing – whatever it is that is happening - is it more serious than I thought?"

"I think so my lady."

"Did you see Beth?"

"Yes, she was the emissary's prisoner. What did she do?"

"Nothing - the emissary is after Daria, another servant of mine. He can have her – too much work that one. He took Beth to identify Daria. I'm hoping to catch up to him and exchange one of my lesser servants for Beth."

"She must be like a daughter to you?"

Lady Kettery glared at her, and said sternly in rebuke: "No one is like a daughter to me! She is an excellent seamstress. That is all!"

"Very well, my lady," the Duchess said demurely, remembering the stubborn woman's pride. "If you have any chance of getting her back, you must get to the emissary before he leaves Baywood."

Suddenly the Duchess dropped the volume in her voice as if someone might hear them. "There is something happening my lady. I don't dare ask the duke, but there is talk I pick up on – enemies are on the move."

"What enemies?" Lady Kettery asked in a normal tone.

"I don't know," answered the Duchess still speaking softly. "Our Baron is somehow involved. He is missing."

"So I've heard. Whatever is going on is of no interest to me. I just want my seamstress back. That is why after a quick lunch we resume our journey."

"But not on that wagon my lady! You will never get there in time. Are any of you riders?"

"I am but have not ridden in a while. The others have no experience."

"Then I will assign four men to carry you swiftly to Baywood. Leave your trunks here and get them on your return."

"It is quite kind of you to do this," Lady Kettery said. "It will greatly increase our chances of finding the emissary."

"Even so, do not get your hopes too high my lady."

"I don't hope...I take."

*

Daria had arrived in Baywood on her third day after leaving Dogwood. She inquired about a reputable inn, which for a girl traveling alone meant safety. At dawn Daria went to one of the stables and sold the steed she made off with for twenty quib. Pleased with the sale of the horse, the rest of the journey to Wilderwood would be by ship.

Daria liked the subtle rocking motion of the vessel as she looked out over the great blue expanse. It was soothing, relaxing. Baywood was nearly out of sight. She breathed a sigh of relief. The teenage girl had evaded the palace guard. She determined by the time she arrived in Wilderwood the emissary would have since given up searching for her.

The hours passed slowly, though Daria didn't mind. The sun had just vanished below the horizon while she stood gazing at pinkish-violet clouds shaped as narrow slats against an indigo backdrop ascending to a dark twilight high above. She cherished the moment. In Fartherwood one could rarely enjoy such a sunset with the tall confining trees.

Along the shore was a string of villages with the soft glow of candlelight emanating from small windows. She thought of her friend Beth, warm and safe in their room in the manor. She was where she belonged.

*

"Woe," Kai hollered, his horse quickly coming to a stop. The dust rose into Beth's nostrils.

"We'll spend the night here," said Page as he dismounted in front of the Baywood Stay.

"Kai, you and Baker line us up passage on a ship for Driftwood tomorrow."

"Yes, my lord," Kai said scurrying off with Baker at his heels.

"Maybe Daria is still here in Baywood," Page said to Beth. "If so, she too will be at the crowded harbor first thing tomorrow. If you see her, tell us. If you do, it will go well for you both. I know that Daria is not directly involved, but I need to find Harbinger."

"Yes, my lord," said Beth, "I know your word is good."

Beth awoke just before dawn. She remained in her comfortable riding clothes that the Duchess had given her. As Beth rolled over she felt a few large coins she wasn't aware of that must have been placed there by the duchess which must have been worth 25 quib a piece!

Beth wondered what this meant. She was a mere servant girl and the Duchess was one of the most powerful women in Fartherland. It could simply be an act of kindness, but an act of kindness towards a stranger would only warrant a few quib - not this much. Beth believed it was more than benevolence. The Duchess had taken a liking to her because of her interest in the embroidery on her dress and the forthcoming of her ability as an adroit seamstress.

Then a comforting notion dawned on her. Could the Duchess desire her to work in Dogwood? When all this was over, was the money to pay for her expense back to the castle. Yet Beth recalled that the emissary had told Lady Kettery that he would return her seamstress back to the manor once Daria was caught. And that would end any hope of working for the Duchess.

Beth closed her eyes to the inevitable. She would be returned to Fartherwood. Suddenly Beth's eyes flashed open in anger. What was she - some commodity to be used and shuffled around for the sake of the needs of others? She was a person with desires and feelings and dreams of her own, and her dream now was to work for the Duchess.

Beth got a glimpse of Daria's headstrong personality. Daria was not happy as a seamstress and feared not for her own safety. Beth then realized by her friend's action that change can only come about through risk, and here was a risk she was now willing to accept.

Beth looked around. The emissary had moved his bed against the door, blocking any hope of sneaking out that way; and Kai slid his bed in front of the only window so in order to climb out she would have to crawl over Kai without waking him up…impossible.

Just as Beth was ready to resign herself to her predictable fate she noticed that Kai had opened the shutter a crack before he settled down for the night to allow in some cool air. A plan started to formulate in her head. She ran it through her mind a few times until confident it had a chance of working. Beth crawled softly to Kai's bed and picked up his sword within its scabbard.

While she held it out over the bed her arms shook under the strain of the weight, her sleeve caressed prickly goose bumps and she suddenly wondered: *What am I doing? I will be caught, ashamed, disgraced, and punished. I am not Daria!*

Without being aware of her own movements the tip of the scabbard caught the bottom of the shutter. She automatically drew it her way, and the shutter swung open. It was done. Beth then gently lowered the heavy weapon back on the floor and looked at her trembling hands. Her mind raced back to the last time she had done something that was not out of duty or a command or a desire of someone else. She could not recall.

She immediately went into action, her mind and body now responding naturally to the crisis she had created. She grabbed her bag and cape and crawled beneath a few extra blankets the men had tossed off the beds in a heap on the floor. Beth curled herself in a womb-like position beneath the inconspicuous pile and waited. Although the young seamstress was conscious of her scary predicament, she felt embolden.

As she waited beneath the blankets trying to remain motionless her burst of power and courage elapsed into petrified fright. In her mind's eye she saw them searching the room and then coming upon the blankets they pulled them off revealing a ball of shivering flesh as the men roared in laughter at her pathetic attempt at escape.

She then heard some movement above.

The emissary woke to a cold draft blowing in the window along with the sounds of the harbor slowly coming to life. Though the room was still dark, the gray dawn was visible outside. "Baker, wake up," the emissary ordered, rocking the knight. "Wake the girl."

Page turned toward Kai who was snoring intermittently, and spoke somewhat annoyed, "Kai, enough sleep. Now close the window. It is cold in here!"

"She's gone!" said Baker. He then dropped to his knees. "She's not under the beds!"

"The window," gasped the emissary. He looked over at Kai who was still groggy. "Wake up, Kai!" the emissary ordered sternly.

"Yes, my lord," Kai said, wondering why the earnest command.

"She's gone…escaped out the window!"

"That's impossible! She could not have escaped without waking me up."

"I called to you twice just now because you didn't hear me the first time."

"But…"

Page interrupted in a reprimanding tone. "Never mind, she probably just left or we would have awoken much earlier to that stiff breeze blowing in off the water - or should I say Baker and I would have. Come, both of you!" the emissary said as they followed him out the room. "Kai, round up some knights in the city to aid us. We need to keep these ships from sailing until we have time to search for the damn woman."

Baker shivered and asked as they exited the inn into the chill of early dawn, "Do you think she has the money for passage to Driftwood?"

"I'm not going to assume she doesn't."

Beth, like some winter animal ascending from its borough, slowly stuck her head out from her hiding. It had worked, but now what. Her plan went no further than this. She crawled to the window and saw the hubbub her escape had caused. She thought the safest place for now was to remain in the room, but suddenly Beth realized the chamber maids would be coming in soon to prepare the room for the next guest. She went to the common room. The innkeeper recognized her as the young lady with the emissary.

"Good morning," Beth said, "the emissary told me to tell you we will be staying another night." She reached in her pocket and pulled out 25 quib and paid the man. "Wait here," he said, not taken aback that this girl who accompanied the emissary would be carrying a coin of large value.

When he returned with her change, she smiled and gave a slight nod and went back to the room and waited for an opportune time to leave.

*

By midmorning the knights the emissary could muster were searching the ships at the far end of the harbor. Beth assumed that the emissary would also be in that vicinity as well. *I must leave now.* Beth changed back into the dress she wore from Fartherwood and along with her cape would blend in more with the attire of the woman folk. She grabbed her bag stuffed with her riding clothes and left the room. Beth put her hood up as she stepped outside. She walked along the store fronts and guild shops until she came to a street that led into the city proper.

The road was a steep incline. The better part of the city rested on the side of a hill which gazed down upon the bustling harbor. When she came to an establishment called The Sea Crest

Inn, she went inside and registered for the night under the name of Alianor.

It was late afternoon when the weary emissary and his two knights opened the door to the common room and entered the Baywood Stay. He approached the owner. "We'll be staying another night." Page pulled eight quib out of his pocket.

"There is no need to pay twice," the proprietor said.

"What are you talking about?"

"The young woman that is with you paid earlier for another night my lord."

Page glanced at the other two and then at the owner. "Is she in there now?"

"I do not know. I have not seen her since this morning."

"Thank you sir, I did not realize she had paid our bill, goodnight."

Kai closed the door of their room. "I knew she did not climb out the window. She was here all along, right under our noses."

"But where?" asked Baker. "I had looked under the beds."

Page walked over to the spare blankets crumpled on the floor and lifted them up. Page then looked at his knights who gazed at the blank space on the floor, bewildered how the meek and mild Beth could outwit them just as Daria had.

Page spoke solemnly: "Beth knew she was not in any trouble, was under no reprimand, was to receive no punishment and that her life would resume its normalcy once Daria was found. I am afraid we have underestimated the scroll and all those involved with it, but no more. Kai, check and see if all of our horses are still in the stable."

The palace guard hurriedly left the room.

"So, Baker, where would you go if you were her?"

"The Duchess seemed to take a liking to her. Perhaps she is going back to Dogwood."

"I disagree...too dangerous. The Duchess, no matter what her feelings for Beth, if any, would not accept Beth into her household without written consent from Lady Kettery. Beth probably knows this. No, she's biding her time somewhere in the city. She's going to Driftwood to look for Daria."

"What about making her way back to Lady Kettery in Fartherwood?"

"That is a possibility if we are missing a horse, but I have a feeling they are all there."

Baker turned when he heard footsteps rushing down the hall. Kai burst into the room puffing. "All our horses are accounted for," the knight stated.

"I guess that rules out Fartherwood, my lord," said Baker. "She's not going to walk back, which leaves us with your scenario."

"Which is what?" asked Kai trying to catch up.

"She's here Kai," said Page, "somewhere in Baywood. She's biding her time, waiting for a safe opportunity to board a ship for Driftwood, and if an opportunity is what she wants, an opportunity is what she'll get. We will remove the presence of the knights from the harbor tomorrow. The three of us will choose unassuming locations and wait and watch. Perhaps one of us will notice the redhead looking for passage to Driftwood."

"But perhaps not my lord," said Kai, "then what? We cannot recognize Daria."

"Then we leave the following morning for Wilderwood. Remember, Kingsley travels with Merrill to Wilderwood. Even if Daria and Beth make it that far unhindered, they are unaware that Kingsley has sided with us. He can recognize them."

"I would rather find them before that," Merrill said, more annoyed now since even the docile Beth had eluded them.

"It seems," said Baker, "those two girls are deeply involved as well. What is in that scroll?"

"What indeed?" asked Page.

2

The Family

Beth lay awake the following morning trying to comprehend the stupid thing she had done. If caught, this impetuous action may get her in deeper trouble than she imagined. Was the emissary ordering a search of all the inns in Baywood as she lay here under the false security that she had outwitted him? Beth now realized she had overreacted when she found those coins. She wondered to herself how one scenario could seem so plausible one day and the next day viewed as great folly.

Beth got dressed, went out to the common room, and sat. She relaxed a little as the heat emanating from the large central hearth began edging out the dampness. The logical scenario kept playing in her head – find the emissary and surrender; admit of her foolish error and play the part of a frightened teenage girl which wouldn't require much acting anyway. The emissary seemed lenient in reasonable situations. His urgency to find Daria might waive any punishment she would rightfully deserve – at least temporarily. Her mind was made up. She believed it was not too late to reverse the damage she had done if she moved swiftly.

The proprietor called out behind the desk to a well-dressed gentleman who sat at a trestle table near her. "Sidon, how is the Duke of Dogwood these days?"

Beth looked over at the well-dressed merchant sitting at table hunched over a few scrolls, absorbed, unaware of anyone else in the room. He glanced up and answered, "Some trifle going on about the Baron missing. I have no details, but I will enquire. Baron Durkel is wily and unpredictable, probably off on some lucrative venture he wants to keep veiled. By the way, I must be going. The time has escaped me." The merchant began rolling up his scrolls.

Beth, who a moment ago had resolved herself of her next move, now reconsidered. She had plenty of money and now the means lie before her to get to Dogwood without much fuss since this man was on his way there on business. The only question was how the Duchess would receive her – if at all. But even if nothing came of it, she had plenty of money to resume her trip back to Fartherwood and the Kettery manor. Beth approached the merchant before she had a reason to once again reconsider.

"Pardon, my lord," Beth began, "I overheard you saying you know the Duke of Dogwood. I know him too. Well, I should say the Duchess more so."

"Yes, we've cooperated on a couple of ventures together. Get to the point! I have to go."

"I would like passage with you. I can easily pay my way my lord."

"Very well, there's still some room. You pay one half when we commence and the rest when we arrive."

"Yes, my lord."

"Give me six quib. Come, we must hurry," the merchant remarked tersely. "I'm running late. You have everything."

"Yes, my lord, just this satchel."

"Then follow me." Sidon walked quickly out the door. He was tall and his strides were long. Beth had to walk at a clip to keep up. The weather was misty. She was glad. She pulled the hood of her cape over her head to conceal her flaming red hair. Beth expected a short hike to the stable to board his wagon, but the tall man kept descending the narrow winding roads. Soon she felt the bite of a cool sea breeze and the sounds of men's voices shouting orders. She was afraid to ask him anything. His face was fixed straight ahead. They rounded a corner and before her was the harbor.

Beth wondered what he was doing. Then she relaxed when she realized his workers would be loading his wagon with goods from one of the ships. She hoped it was already done, and they could immediately board the wagon and be on their way to Dogwood.

They walked out into the open area of the docks. She knew the emissary and the knights would be watching for a woman her height, but alone. She now walked close, nearly leaning against the tall man.

"There it is come," he ordered as he walked toward a long boat.

What is this! We're heading toward a ship.

"Good day Sidon," one of the deck hands said cheerfully as the tall man boarded. Too late – she could not go back. She may have been spotted by the emissary, though with this wealthy merchant she would be dismissed as his traveling companion. She dare not leave his side.

On board Beth noticed a family of four sitting down making ready for the passage. She asked, "Excuse me, where is this ship going?"

The husband answered, "Driftwood."

Beth's jaw dropped. Her impulsive decision had put her standing worse off than before. She plunked herself down behind some barrels and faced the open sea. The brisk breeze, the expanse of the vast blueness of the water was exhilarating; yet this was not what she wanted. No matter how hard she tried to break away she kept getting pulled further into this mess.

*

The bay was socked in with fog at the close of the day. The emissary and his two knights who had spent the day in wait for Beth now stood together on one of the piers.

"So now what?" asked Baker. "I saw no one who matched Beth's description."

"Nor I," said Page despondently, "you, Kai?"

"There was a short woman but she was with a tall distinguished gentleman. I enquired who he was. I was told

he is a wealthy merchant from Driftwood. He owns his own
ship and occasionally makes regular trips between Baywood and
Driftwood, so it couldn't have been her."

"Instead of expending the energy to find out who he was, why
didn't you simply check to see if it was Beth?" Page exclaimed,
somewhat exhausted from his knight's incompetence.

"I'm sure it wasn't her."

"How can you be sure? Come!"

The two knights followed the emissary off the dock toward
the Baywood Stay. The innkeeper was in the common room.
"Tell me," said Page directly. Then he turned to Kai. "What
was his name?"

"Sidon."

"Tell me," repeated Page to the proprietor, "have you heard
of him?"

"I should say I have. He has frequented here."

"On his trips to Driftwood does he allow passengers looking
for route there?"

"I should say so my lord. And he doesn't gouge them either
- charges a fair price."

"Did you hear that Kai! He takes on passengers and charges
a fair price!"

"But, my lord…"

It was Baker though who answered. "My lord, we can't be
sure. The chances are…"

"Yes, yes I know. The chances are it wasn't her. But still in
our desperate situation any slight lead needed to be examined"
Page turned and glared at Kai and then to the owner, said, "We'll
have some ale."

The three men shuffled over to a table and plunked themselves
down in a chair. No one spoke.

*

The four horsemen issued by the Duchess of Dogwood
bearing Lady Kettery, Ursula, Driscoll, and Blackrose trotted
through the thick fog that appeared to be draped like a white

sopping veil over the port city of Baywood. Only the occasional blurry light from an oil lamp penetrated the misty curtain. Not even the cobblestones the horses clacked upon could be seen, giving the four horses an illusion of prancing through the air.

It was a welcomed relief when the four horsemen reined in their horses outside of an inn called the Baywood Stay. Lady Kettery led her weary ragtag crew inside and approached the owner who was glancing down at his ledger. She asked bluntly, "Was the emissary here?"

"He is here, in his room."

She glanced over at her servants. "Driscoll and Blackrose, here are some coins. Register two rooms. And my good sir," Lady Kettery said to the innkeeper, "would you please inform the emissary that Lady Kettery is here to see him. He'll come."

"Yes, my lady," he abruptly responded and hurried down the hallway.

"Sit," she said to Ursula.

"Poor Blackrose," Ursula said quietly to her mistress. "She does not suspect a thing, completely unaware that she will be traded off for Beth, but we both agree it is for the best."

"Everything I do is for the best…my best."

Baker responded to a knock on their door. "Yes," he answered, opening it a crack.

"A Lady Kettery here to see the emissary," spoke the voice from the hallway.

Page jerked back the door quickly. "Lead the way"

Page noticed the elderly woman and one of her servants sitting at a small table. "Thank you my good man," Page said to the man who had summoned him.

Lady Kettery and Ursula both stood as Page approached the table. "Please sit my lady. And you too," he said to Ursula who remained standing.

Page noticed the grime and fatigue from travelers only accustomed to short bouts to a nearby village. "And what brings you so far from home my lady."

"I have come for Beth. I am quite willing to make an exchange for her with another servant who is taller than Beth and could easily recognize Daria in a crowd."

Ursula looked at her mistress oddly. *Blackrose is a fraction taller than Beth. Why does she lie to the emissary? How far will that get her?*

"To my great chagrin," said Page, "Beth has escaped."

Lady Kettery's draw dropped.

"I know it is hard to believe, but we underestimated her prowess."

"Beth has no prowess!" exclaimed Lady Kettery in disbelief. "The thought of escaping would not even occur to her."

"It did my lady and she has. The scroll is moving many to do things they normally would not do. I need to find out why."

"Where would she even go?" Lady Kettery asked truly puzzled.

"We think Driftwood."

Lady Kettery blew out a despondent sigh as she gathered her thoughts. She quickly formed an alternative plan, cleared her throat, and began: "My lord, since I was a girl, I held a deep love for my kingdom and our brave knights who have defended us against the Barman's to the East. Fartherwood has been kept safe from every direction. Our lives are secure, and our hearts are quieted from all fear because of the diligent action of the knights of the Realm."

Where is this taking us?

"And now I humbly submit to you a small token in return for all you have done for me and all the people of Fartherland. In place of Beth who has denied her service to the Realm I submit to you my servant Ursula."

Ursula looked at her mistress in shock and was speechless.

"That is a most generous offer my lady," said the emissary well aware that he could just seize the servant from her. "When we find Daria, your handmaid will be escorted back to you, and you will be rewarded for your service."

"I will of course graciously accept your reward, but my motivation is not that."

"That is why I hold it out to you my lady. Your selflessness is evident."

Enough pleasantries thought Lady Kettery. She had to leave while all was in her favor. "Thank you, my lord," she said and turned toward Ursula. "You know we'll all be waiting for you to return from your service. Do the emissary well as you have done to me all these years."

Ursula just sat in silence quietly absorbing the treachery. She had been set up all along. Blackrose was never the intended exchange. The subdued wench was a decoy. Ursula did not even glance back at her mistress as she left the table with the emissary.

Lady Kettery knocked on Driscoll's door and belted out, "Come with me!" She led him to her room where Blackrose sat patiently staring at the door like a dog anticipating his master. "Sit," Lady Kettery ordered. Driscoll sat on the edge of a bed by a small round table where a candle burned.

"We did not get Beth. She of all people has escaped the incompetent emissary, but we got rid of Ursula…at least for a time. I have been thinking. We shall return home the long way, by way of Driftwood. The emissary believes that is where Beth was heading. The girl is not herself. Swiftly catapulted from her safe environment she is lost and frightened, not acting sensibly."

Lady Kettery noticed Driscoll's dismayed look. She then shot a glance at Blackrose and addressed them. "You both are new to the manor, so I should not expect you to know this but know it from here on. We are like a family. We watch out for each other. Is that understood?"

"It is as you say, my lady," Blackrose said meekly. "It is a comfort to know that."

Driscoll sat quietly pretending not to notice this hidden character flaw in his mistress. Putting oneself out of sorts for the sake of another who was expendable he saw as the first sign in a person's downfall.

Lady Kettery jolted Driscoll from his reverie. "Then it is settled. We leave tomorrow for Driftwood, not as if I need your consent, but it is good that we all agree…as a family."

3
Driftwood

The next morning Driscoll looked on from the docks as the ship the emissary boarded sailed out of the bay. "They're gone," he said in finality, "along with Ursula. You are to be commended my lady."

Lady Kettery did not respond but spoke distantly, "You've got some big shoes to fill."

"But my lady," he said surprised at the remark, "you said Ursula could not be trusted, that she was a thorn in your side."

"She was that and more, but at the end of the day she took care of things in spite of herself. I hope you can do the same."

"Of course, my lady, you will not be disappointed."

"We shall see," she said. "Now we'll split up and look for a ship with the lowest fare. Meet back here in an hour."

*

Blackrose sat on a crate clustered around several others as Lady Kettery returned from one direction and Driscoll from the other.

"What have you got?" Lady Kettery asked Blackrose who sat up straight, her back stiff as a board, her posture perfect.

"Twenty quib my lady."

"For how many?" she asked with a smirk knowing it could not be for them all.

"All of us, of course, my lady."

"That's impossible! What did you do to secure that fair?"

"I told him how much I would pay. He said that is acceptable."

"That is clearly an unacceptable amount," Driscoll asserted. "Even a novice sea hand would recognize that."

"He is right," Lady Kettery said in firm agreement. "Anyone would know that is far too low. What did you do to secure such a fare?"

"I have a way with words my lady," Blackrose said in a meek yet commanding tone which took them both by surprise, yet they could do nothing but submit to it, and the thought of any more questioning left them.

"Of course you do," Lady Kettery humbly stated.

"Indeed," parroted Driscoll.

"When does it leave?" Lady Kettery asked.

"In two hours."

"Good, that will give the emissary some distance between us." Lady Kettery glanced over at Driscoll who had turned from them both and meandered down to the edge of the dock and wondered how she could have beat him. He had haggled excessively to get a low price of 28 quib. Between sudden unexpected feelings for Ursula which Lady Kettery harbored and now with this undemonstrative nubile upstart his path to head servant would not be as easy as first imagined. Driscoll believed that in time Ursula would be forgotten but that subdued young wench was someone to be reckoned with.

*

The ship bearing Daria hugged the southern shore of Fartherland. She stood gripping the gunwale facing the stern, and a strong westerly wind blew her hair back like a flag proudly pronouncing its identity to the world. The sharp slap of the waves against the hull echoed in Daria's ears, and she swayed side to side with the rhythmic up/down motion of the ship. It was making good time as it plowed head long towards Driftwood.

Everything was going according to plan. Yet there was a faint sound in her conscious as a gentle knock upon a door, a small voice yet with an urgent message: *'This is not the way.'*

Why this sudden disturbance? All is well. Leave me alone!

Daria let go of the gunwale and in defiance the teenage girl swirled around and squinted as the low sunlight reflected off a high circular wall of white marble. "Look at that?" she gasped, dazzled by the opulent spectacle and that small voice faded into obscurity.

A mother of four who stood by her side, spoke gruffly, "Never seen Driftwood before, eh?"

"No," said Daria unapologetically.

"It is a city for the wealthy. If a poor person desires to live there, they must agree to be someone's slave for life. Even then, stringent requirements are demanded for slaves."

"It doesn't look like any other place in Fartherland."

"That is because it is not from Fartherland."

"What do you mean?" Daria asked, snappishly. "That makes no sense."

"It is a floating island."

"Islands don't float," Daria stated abrasively, remembering that Glendyland folks are steeped in superstitions – a harbor for witches and warlocks, a people given unto magic potions and spells.

"This one floats or should I say used to. For the last two hundred years it has been grounded here in the mouth of the River Green where it has become an important trade city. It is now the wealthiest port in the Realm. But the alchemists say that the river has been inching the island back out to sea over the last one hundred years, and soon it will break away again and float elsewhere."

Daria glanced back at the city. There was a dock which encircled the white walls. She counted four ships unloading goods. As her ship sailed to starboard a large open gate came into view, and she caught a glimpse behind the walls. The attire of the folks was bright and exuberant - the colors of prosperity and leisure.

The sailors lowered the sails and the rowers took to guiding the ship towards the piers. Daria grew excited as a couple of sailors set the plank in place to allow the passengers to debark.

The road was broad which led into the city and was covered with stone pavers. *No muddy ruts here – so much cleaner!* The buildings on both sides of the street were three, some four stories high with huge water basins on the roof to collect rain water for drinking. The marbled exterior walls varied in pastel colors, and the front facades differed in design giving some a bold clean look of authority while others boasted frilly ornate fascia and others with excessive sculpted scenes of animals, warriors, and gods and demons in animated confrontations.

Daria noticed much hubbub as she approached an impressive city square. There were several guilds exhibiting their goods from different lands, articles strange and unfamiliar to Daria. As she took in the magnificent structures, the flagrant wealth, the flaunting attire of the folks who dwelt here, she believed she was destined for becoming well-placed with or without Harbinger. She would have liked to have stopped and perused these wares as was the case in Dogwood, but Daria felt light headed and weak. She needed to eat something.

In the far right corner of the square she saw a host of young maidens clustered around what she determined must be tables of vegetables, meats, fish, and fowl. Daria inched her way through a heavy conglomerate of wealthy foreigners who had made Driftwood their home. She went over to one of the tables. "What are these things?" she asked and pointed.

"Avocados," a woman brusquely answered, eyeing her with disdain. Daria noticed the merchant staring at her in disgust and alarm. The young maiden from Fartherwood quickly glanced around and noticed she was totally out of place, a misfit, a deviation. There were only two classes of people wherever she looked. The well to-do and slaves, but even the slaves were clean and well dressed in a simple style set by the city council so that there would be a clear demarcation, leaving no excuse for social mingling.

Daria glanced down and noticed how filthy her dress was. She then realized her hair also was stringy and dirty. She raised her head and saw in their eyes that she was more than an odd figure but an abscess, a mutation within their walls.

The woman spoke and said curtly, "She doesn't belong here! She is not one of us, and she is not one of them!" She raised her voice and cried for help so to cut the malignancy out before it could spread.

A portly gentleman stepped over. "Is this girl harassing you, Ayleth?"

"Is not her very presence harassment enough?"

Daria glared hard at the tubby man.

"Oh! This one is a feisty one. I like them feisty." He grabbed Daria's forearm.

With a sudden jerk she pulled her arm free and ran shoving and pushing her way through the throng in the square. When she glanced back, she saw the man did not follow. Daria looked around at the strange faces. Most of them glared at her the same way. Out of the corner of her eyes she noticed a man who seemed to have a kind face. "Good sir," she said politely drawing his attention.

"A new slave, huh? Looking for the upper canal?"

"Yes, my lord," Daria said playing along.

"Too bad you're spoken for."

Oh no, not him too. "My lord – the upper canal – which way?"

"What does he pay? I'll pay more!"

"Thank you, my lord, I'll find my own way." She dashed from the man with the kind face. When out of range she stopped to get her baring. Daria's attention was drawn upward towards the dark clouds rolling in. The sun had now set behind the walls of the city, increasing her anxiety in this foreign and strange place. The affluent denizens now scurried around her as a colony of ants while she stood motionless, their bright colored clothes fading in brilliance, blending into the gray shadows of dusk.

She would find the upper canal herself and seek refuge there. She walked at a crisp clip avoiding eye contact. The lavish buildings continued beyond the square. She noticed a boy and a girl hurrying along. The boy lugged a leather satchel over his shoulder filled with something heavy. He had a look of destitution as if punishment awaited him for perhaps being late. The girl briskly walked by the boy without even a glance or concern of his predicament. She bore the same fear in her eyes as the boy. By their garb it appeared that the slaves were well treated but apparently they were not.

Daria then realized how hot tempered and demeaning Lady Kettery was at times, but all her servants were taken care of. In her own way she seemed to watch out for them – not so here. The slaves were looked upon as dogs yet the aristocracy perceived themselves as doing them a favor for the privilege of serving them.

The young girl turned right. Daria followed. The road was long and straight just as the previous one. Farther ahead was a bridge. Daria glanced down at her dirty dress and ran her fingers through her greasy hair. The romance of an adventure was over as the grayish light of dusk began to recede into darkness. She continued towards the bridge. Other smaller streets shot off the wide road she traversed, each one running straight without any bends. She determined the city was set up like a chess board.

The canal which passed through the city was fed by the River Green. It was an expanse of not more than fifty feet, yet Daria could see that life on the other side was a far cry from the place where she stood. But she was not accepted over here, and now she wasn't sure if she would be accepted over there.

When she stepped onto the other side, it seemed like a world away. The buildings were blocks of mismatched rock. The whole area was dingy looking and everything was dirty. The slaves had no energy or time to take care of their own environment. What little time they had to themselves was spent on survival.

The streets here were not laid out in a grid but ran haphazardly. The road ended in an open square, though not nearly as large as the one on the other side. The square backed up to the wall of the city. There was a large gate which led to the circular dock which enveloped the walls of the city. The gate was open. Daria looked out onto the river and the forest beyond to the mainland which maintained the last fragment of twilight. It seemed so near, but the current at the mouth of the river was strong and impossible to swim against so that no guards were needed to keep the slaves behind the walls.

Her eye caught a table with some bruised fruit, but edible nevertheless. The girl across from her looked at her and smiled. She seemed approachable. The girl bought some green beans and immediately left. Daria paid for her fruit which price she thought was a little excessive, though only for the fact that nearly everything had to be shipped in daily.

Daria pursued the girl. "Excuse me," Daria said politely, "could you direct me toward an inn."

"An inn?" the thin maiden said. "There are no inns here. No one visits the upper canal. You must be new. Haven't you been assigned a room yet?"

"I am not a slave," Daria said somewhat insulted. "I am just passing through Driftwood. I'm leaving tomorrow. I just need a place for the night. The rooms are very expensive in the city. I'll pay you something for your hospitality."

Daria noticed that the maiden looked shocked. "You are a free woman?"

"Yes," Daria said as if it should have been obvious.

"I would be honored then if you stayed with me. My name is Puah."

"I'm Daria."

"Come, Daria, this way."

Puah left the square and turned down a narrow side street, then up to the second floor of a long building. The hallway was dark with minimal light from two candles on each end. Puah opened a door to a small room. "This is my home," she said to Daria rather proudly.

Daria's eyes scanned the shadowed dwelling. Puah opened the shutters of the only window. Daria saw but three feet away a wall of another building backed up to this one. Puah lit here only candle. There was enough light to see how homey Puah had made her room. It was clean and tastefully decorated with things no doubt she must have found. There was only one bed, though Daria did not mind sleeping on the floor. She would be safe here and warm. Just then she heard some rain drops falling into the alley…and dry.

Daria put the food she had bought on the table. Puah was thrilled by a scrumptious dinner which would consist of more than a few green beans and said, "The gods have truly smiled upon me today."

Daria did not want to disrupt the girl's joy but this seemed hardly a meal to rejoice over. "I'm happy for you," Daria said, though wondering why these poor slaves didn't just simply board the first ship leaving Driftwood to anywhere. As she pondered this thought she felt her dwindling supply of remaining monies in her purse. She was beginning to realize that poverty itself was enslavement.

After they ate, Puah spread a blanket on the floor and lay down. "What are you doing?" asked Daria.

"I am exhausted," she answered. "I must sleep now."

"Yes, of course, but in your bed!"

"Oh no, Daria – I have not eaten so much food in one sitting like this for a long time. The gods have been good to me today. I dare not upset them."

Daria knew if the gods had smiled upon anyone, it was her. She was safe, warm, and dry in this hostile environment because of this poor slave who kindly opened her home to her. Yet Daria would not remove this girl's joy by insisting that she sleep in her own bed. Daria took a spare blanket and tucked it around Puah. The slave smiled warmly with her eyes closed.

I will not forget this girl's kindness.

4
Wilderwood

Daria's eyes flashed open. She quickly raised her head and looked around at the unfamiliar dark space. She had been in a deep sleep, and for an instant she forgot where she was. Daria flung off the covers of the bed in a panic, frightened in the strange surrounding. She noticed the blankets on the floor and breathed a sigh of relief. It was the spot where the slave girl slept. Puah was gone. Daria opened the shuttered window. Indirect light poured in. *The rain is over. How long have I slept. I've got to get out of this city...find a ship...hurry!*

She glanced into her purse, and although she would need every last quib to reach her destination, she nevertheless left a token for Puah. Her heart told her to leave more but her mind said no, she had to first think of herself.

The gate in the small market square was open. Daria exited onto the dock. She followed the circular platform around the white walls of the city inquiring at each ship if they were on their way to Wilderwood...no luck. She sat on a bench facing west and looked out along the southern shore of Fartherland. She saw a speck in the distance. The speck grew. It was a ship.

Daria patiently waited. It tied up at one of the piers which jutted out from the circular dock. The travelers departed first. Daria noticed a short redhead. *That looks like Beth. It is Beth! What is she doing here?*

Daria ran down the pier. Beth noticed her friend's frizzy blond hair blowing wildly around her head from the brisk sea breeze. "Daria!" she cried out. Daria stopped and pushed her hair above her high forehead and waved. Beth ran towards her and the two hugged.

"How have you come to be here?" Daria asked excitedly.

"It is a long story, and I will tell you about it but not now. We need to find a ship leaving for Wilderwood. The emissary is not far behind."

"I assumed he chose the Northern Way."

"I'll explain the whole thing later."

"You might as well tell me now. None of the ships presently docked are going upriver. We must wait. Tell me everything. Here, sit."

"Very well," Beth said. The two girls sat on the bench Daria had just vacated. It was a thick white marble seat with an elevated arched back and high arms which curled out at the top affording some protection from the winds off the Midland Sea.

Beth sat with her legs tight together and rubbed her hands along her lap as if to take the wrinkles from her dirty dress. Daria sat with her legs crossed as if she were a world traveler waiting for her next ship to tend to her busy life, but to a passerby both appeared weary and out of place, unaccustomed to life on the run.

Upon finishing the episode of her impetuous plan of escape to Dogwood, she concluded, "I had thought after you left the manor, I would be left alone, that my life would get back to normal…I was wrong."

"So what are you going to do," Daria asked?

"My plans have not changed. I am going to Dogwood, but I've got to keep ahead of the emissary. When I get to Wilderwood, I will connect with someone heading west along the Northern Way."

"My plans are not so definite," Daria said with a twinge of jealousy. Her friend seemed to have a good future lined up. Daria's good future was dependent on Harbinger's future which now seemed questionable. "We can at least travel together to Wilderwood."

At that moment Sidon strode by in his hurried familiar gait. He stopped not far from the two young maidens and spoke hastily to another merchant. "Gilford, my vessel is too big for the river. May I hire out the use of your boat? You will be compensated well. My men will load my wares upon your smaller craft. I need to stop at Riverwood and then onto Wilderwood."

The burly sailor said nothing but nodded. He knew Sidon well, a fair minded merchant but demanding.

The two women glanced at each other. "Sir," Beth called.

Sidon turned. Beth ran up to him. "I will pay for myself and my friend for passage upriver to Wilderwood."

"Half now…six quib each. We spend tonight in Riverwood. The day after we will arrive in Wilderwood. We part in one hour. We won't wait."

*

The following day the Baron sat alone on a large boulder in the deep forest of Genadar just outside the densely populated village that the giant owl had brought him to. Through the trees he could see some of the ramblings going on. Although he had won the support of the Barbarians on the night of his arrival, since then little progress had been made. It had been eleven days. Communication was the problem.

He heard someone above him. He glanced up from the rock he sat on. It was a tall lissome woman in a tree. Her legs dangled from a slender branch she sat on. The young woman was very attractive but for one odd feature. Her deep brown hair was long and wavy, her eyes sharp with a slight upward angle, her smooth skin perfectly tanned (which seemed odd for one coming out of a cold winter), but it was her wide mouth the Baron noticed which seemed out of place from an otherwise perfectly formed woman. Even so, it came with a welcoming wide smile.

He waved her down. She stood up straight with perfect balance on the thin limb and climbed down. The Baron slid off the outcrop of granite.

She pointed to herself, "Marshstench," she said. She repeated her name and then poked his muscular chest. Durkel simply looked at her finger and then at her questioningly. "Marshstench," she said again and poked the Baron once more harder.

"Oh," he said suddenly enlightened. "She wants to know my name. Durkel," he said pointing at himself.

She smiled.

"It's not much, but it's a start."

The woman then touched the boulder. "Onc," she said. He reached out and placed his big palm on the rock. "Onc," he said to her.

With that broad smile of approval she pressed her hand against the tree. "Thweehart," she pronounced slowly.

"Thweehart," the Baron slowly repeated. At last he was on his way.

*

Another two days had passed and a cursory search by the palace guards in Wilderwood for the remaining men from Fartherwood turned up nothing. The sun had gone down as Merrill, Ewar, Tybalt, and Kingsley stood on the dock at the end of day. A starless sky left the men unable to see, but they could hear the gentle splashing of oars until at last a shape took form appearing out of the blackness over the dark waters.

A ship docked. The passengers got off first. Kingsley noticed Daria and Beth. He tugged on Merrill's sleeve, murmured: "Those two maidens – Daria and Beth."

"They caught Daria," exclaimed Merrill in a lowered but excited tone, "what good fortune!"

Leaning in towards Merrill, Tybalt questioned, "But where is the emissary, Ulric, Kai, and Baker?"

"Are you sure it is them?" asked Merrill in a subdued voice.

Kingsley whispered loudly, "I am sure!"

"Bring them here," Merrill ordered nodding at his two knights.

Daria and Beth stood on First Street glancing up and down for a nearby inn. They did not want to go searching down unfamiliar streets at night. The men's footsteps came from behind. "Looking for a place to stay," said Ewar caustically. "We have one for you. Come this way."

The two girls recognized the raiment of the palace guards.

"Move," Ewar ordered, "that way!" He pointed towards Merrill.

Beth walked silently, trance-like, her head bowed. *All my effort…my daring escape…for nothing.*

Daria walked upright without batting an eye. She recognized Kingsley standing next to the other guard not appearing as a prisoner but a confidant. "And so Kingsley," Daria asked bluntly, "did you turn in Harbinger too?"

"It was his own undoing. He would not cooperate. My hands are clean!"

I finally found Harbinger but what good as it done me.

*

The next morning Ewar and Tybalt escorted Harbinger and Quayfear with their hands bound towards an awaiting boat. The air was warm but still, and tiny black flies hovered in clusters along the water. The guards waved their hands in front of their faces in a manner of annoyance. Harbinger and Quayfear could merely shake their heads back and forth in helpless frustration at the tiny pests that blanketed the riverfront.

The two prisoners stepped into the boat. Ewar glanced over at Harbinger and said with a snicker, "We've got two more prisoners coming with us. I'll get them."

Quayfear glanced at Harbinger. "Franklin and John," he whispered?

Harbinger shrugged his shoulders. "I suppose."

Harbinger noticed it was Daria who stepped out of the inn, her head held high as if she were in charge leading the knights to the boat. Harbinger knew she was innocent of any wrong doing, but her association with him was enough to keep her in their custody. He was surprised to see Beth. Her spirit seemed crushed. He wondered how she got involved but would hear about it eventually.

"Hello," Daria said to Harbinger as if she had been escorted out for a boat ride.

Harbinger nodded. He did not think it a good idea to display any emotion in front of the knights, though he was ecstatic to see that she was unharmed.

"Hello," Quayfear said to her, admiring her beauty in spite of her unkempt appearance. Daria did not respond but assumed him to be one of the Baron's scribes Ursula had mentioned.

She stepped nonchalantly off of the dock and onto the small vessel, but with her hands tied she lost her balance and fell forward onto Harbinger knocking him on his back. "Ow," he cried, hitting the rib of the boat. Harbinger felt her soft slender body sprawled helplessly on his chest and was glad for it. She squirmed to remove herself off of him but was unable. She was not willing to show much desire towards a highly potential knight, who, in a very short time was reduced to a prisoner of the palace guard, now unlikely to give her the future she deserved.

Tybalt climbed aboard, grabbed Daria from behind as if taking a cat by the scruff of its neck and pulled her off him, shoving her down on a bench and then helped Harbinger up. Beth carefully climbed in and sat alongside Daria. The four men designated to row the craft boarded and then finally Ewar. A deck hand untied the boat and gave it a shove. The rowers started upriver towards the fortress of Edgewood.

Once the city was out of sight, Beth admired the extraordinary beauty of the river. She determined it had to be about 150 feet across. The trees which grew along its banks, all with a gentle bend leaned inward as if in honor of the mighty river and the privilege of growing along its periphery. A Great Blue Heron startled her with its six foot wing span silently gliding overhead.

As much a place of solace as it was, it was yet another move of this invisible force dragging her farther from where she wanted to be. She was heading towards the border of the wilderness. Beth wondered what could be next as she looked at the armed guards in the striking silver and blue garb and the muscular rowers breaking the silence of the deep woods with each stroke of their oars pressing against the flowing river.

*

Brandish stared out the window of the Shady Inn thinking about what to do. He heard voices. He cocked his head out the window and saw three young men at the intersection of Tenth Street and the Northern way. Brandish recognized Luther and then saw that Franklin and the boy from the tavern were with him. He leaped down the narrow stairs two at a time and out the front door.

"Look," said Luther seeing a stocky young man running towards them. "It's Brandish...I think."

Brandish stopped abruptly before them, nearly spilling into the group. He spoke excitedly, though puffing a little from the short sprint. "We are all in danger! The palace guard is here in Wilderwood. I saw them enter the city yesterday. Harbinger and Quayfear were in tow – prisoners! Kingsley was with them too, but he was not their prisoner. Kingsley, one by one, is turning you in. And, you, Luther," Brandish added with a sense of foreboding, "I overheard them say that they were on their way to the guild. You were next!"

"It is fortunate," said Franklin, "we have bumped into each other, but shouldn't you have been far from here by now on your way back to the Great City."

"I was on my way back, but when I arrived in Applewood, I sensed that I should not have left my sister to grieve alone. We just lost our mother to an illness. I then decided to return to Fartherwood to stay a while and comfort her, but when I got back, Daria had left - run away. Her best friend Beth told me she was heading for Wilderwood to search for Harbinger, her betrothed. I have not seen her here though, and she was not with the palace guard yesterday."

"That is good news then," said Franklin. "I wonder where they are taking Harbinger and Quayfear," Franklin asked, though more to himself than Brandish.

"I overheard the commander order them to Edgewood, a fortress along the wilderness to await the arrival of the emissary. He was not with his knights. I have been searching sporadically for my sister," he concocted, not wanting to let on that his main focus was on finding him, "but most of my time was spent here, aware that Kingsley could recognize me as well."

Luther's shoulders slumped as his dreams took yet another turn. His situation worsened by the day. "Now where do I go?" He immediately looked at Franklin. "Don't say the halls of the White King, though it seems that fate is pushing me in that direction."

"What direction," questioned Brandish?

Franklin answered, "John and I are going upriver. We're passing through the wilderness by way of the river."

"I see," said Brandish. "It makes sense. At least you can't get lost along the river. But you'll need food."

"John and I shall buy some provisions and a fishing net with the monies I have left, which is precious little. I do not know Luther's plans."

"I will go upriver with you," said Luther lacking any kind of commitment, "at least until I figure out what I am going to do. I can't stay in Wilderwood as long as Kingsley and the palace guard are here."

"What are you going to do Brandish," Franklin asked?

"I do not want to return to The Great City not knowing the fate of my sister, yet I can't stay here either with Kingsley on the prowl. Like Luther I will join you at least for a time."

Franklin gave a satisfied nod.

Brandish thought of this latest turn and wondered: *I was impressed with Sourlip, though somewhat skeptical of the prophet's assistant actual effectiveness; but now having found Franklin and having a sustainable reason to tag along upriver, I can see the prophecy beginning to realign itself to its true course.* He unconsciously rendered a sly smile to himself.

Luther then broke in, an edge of panic in his voice, "What if the palace guard orders the knights at Edgewood to help find us? They will blanket the city, search the inns!"

Good instinct, Franklin reasoned. *His conscience is switching from what he thinks should have been to the present moment...the way things actually are.* "It will probably come to that Luther. We must leave tonight. We will travel through the woods using the cloak of darkness until we are passed the fortress. From there we will trek by daylight up the River Green."

Brandish declared, "I have traversed down to the end of Tenth Street. The road narrows and I was told leads to the fortress."

"Very good, we will collect our monies and with them buy what we can afford."

Brandish volunteered, "I will go and purchase our needs. I have the least chance of being spotted. They're not looking for me."

"Luther and I will wait in hiding on the edge of the forest."

Franklin looked on as the blacksmith started on his errand. He recalled that Brandish was present at the initial reading of the scroll and was now with them. Even Harbinger and Quayfear were here but under unpleasant circumstances. Kingsley, though betraying them all, had arrived as well. In fact they were all in Wilderwood except Driscoll. It almost seemed like this was some sort of planned rendezvous, though the plan was developing from somewhere outside of themselves.

The innkeeper watched them from a window. He was concerned. He wanted no trouble at his inn from possible malefactors. He was relieved to see three of them walk by going towards the end of Tenth Street...but why down there?

5

The Prisoners

For a while no one said anything as the rowers paddled upriver towards Edgewood. Out of boredom or perhaps because these prisoners were young and their appearance masked well the countenance of typical miscreants, one of the rowers spoke up, "What did they do?"

"Murderers," said Ewar, "at least the two men. They butchered five knights of the Realm while they slept. We are not sure how the two women are woven into this malevolent scheme."

"They didn't kill them," Daria broke out defensively.

"Who else could have done it…the Baron…killed his own knights? The emissary thinks so, but he is chasing shadows and so is your friend Kingsley. Don't think that he is doing himself any favors by turning you in. He will never become a knight. He is untrustworthy. He betrayed you all."

Ewar waited for a response from Harbinger, but Harbinger did not appease.

"Nothing to say about your traitorous friend, is there?"

"Let it be," said Tybalt. "We have been assigned to deliver these men safely to Edgewood. Let's just do it."

It was late afternoon when the river craft docked at a small hamlet along the Green. Harbinger glanced up a gradual rise where sat castle Edgewood.

"This way," said Ewar.

The road was wide and well-worn that led from the hamlet to the castle. Harbinger glanced into the quiet woods. It was as if they were at the edge of the inhabited world. What lie beyond this castle? He was intrigued by it.

Daria raised her head at the towering castle before her. She imagined a small remote outpost this far north but not the case. Unlike the decorative eight foot wall that hemmed in castle Dogwood, these walls were high and thick. They were built for war. The gate was opened. One of the guards recognized the garb of the two palace guards and went to get their commander.

Montague approached them saying, "It is a pleasure always to see the presence of the guard this far north, but having done so, I must ask myself what urgent duty brings you here."

"The emissary is on his way to interrogate these prisoners," Tybalt stated.

"I will see that they are bound in a secure cell."

"My lord, the emissary wants them kept in clean dry rooms and wants no chance of sickness to come to them from ill-fitting conditions. He believes there is more to their crime than we know of."

"I will see to it then." He turned to one of his knights, and said, "Take these palace guards to the great hall for some dinner. I will personally tend to these prisoners."

Montague led the way to a tall tower, accompanied by another guard on duty. They started up a winding stairwell. Beth recalled her journey to the top of castle Dogwood. Was this a repeat of that? After several minutes, it seemed so. They passed several doors on the way until finally Montague opened one of them. "Untie the girls," he ordered. A knight obeyed. Daria and Beth entered. They heard the door shut and a large board placed across the outside of the door.

The ascent resumed. Montague stopped. Harbinger and Quayfear's hands were untied and with a brusque shove they were pushed into the room. Harbinger heard the heavy board put into place. He walked over to the small arched window and stared outdoors. It faced north and had a commanding view of the river. The forest outside the walls had been cleared all the way to the riverbank, giving their enemy no cover or protection from a hail of arrows descending from the walls.

Quayfear sat. "This is turning out to be quite an adventure," the scribe said. "I think I've already had enough for a lifetime."

Harbinger did not respond but considered what strange events had brought them to the gateway of the wilderness. He then spoke, "Our adventure may just be beginning."

*

Daria walked over to the window in her small room which faced south. She could see a distance downriver. The emissary would be here soon, yet her only crime was an attempt to find Harbinger, her betrothed. Daria's immediate concern was Beth. She did not even peer out the window. She just sat silently, embittered by this latest development.

Daria stated gently, "Do not despair. Your stay here is temporary."

Beth resumed her silence.

Daria continued: "I know you are only here because of me. You were absconded to the emissary's side to identify me. Well, I have been caught. You no longer serve any purpose to the emissary. Your escape did not thwart his plans in the least. I see no reason for him to keep you here. You still have enough money to pay for voyage back to Baywood and from there to Dogwood to serve the Duchess."

Beth finally spoke. Daria noticed a flinch of hope in her voice. "It may be as you say, but right now I would be content with simply returning to the manor."

"Of course that is an option too," Daria added in an upbeat manner. "Soon you will be free to do as you please."

"It seems ever since this scroll thing has come to Fartherwood I have not been able to do as I please."

Raising her eyebrows and in an encouraging tone, Daria added, "Do not fret. You will be cut loose from this scroll thing. It gives me comfort to know that you, my dear friend, and my brother are free of this mess."

"Brandish may not be free of it."

"What do you mean?" Daria asked alarmed. "He is by now back in The Great City."

"He might not be."

"What!" Daria exclaimed, flabbergasted that her brother may still be around.

"Shortly after you left an old man came to our work station upstairs. He called himself the prophet."

"The one Brandish had been waiting for?"

"Yes," the prophet asked Brandish's whereabouts. "I told him he had left Fartherwood a few days ago. Then he asked for you."

"Why me?" she asked squinting in wonder at this strange revelation.

"He didn't say. Anyway he told me to give Brandish a message if he returned. I asked him, 'Why would he return? He just left.' But Brandish returned that night."

"Why did he come back?"

"He was worried about you."

Daria smiled warmly. "He is a good brother. What was the message the prophet had for him?"

"Go to Wilderwood and follow Franklin the scribe from Dogwood. Your brother let me know in no uncertain terms he was not happy with the prophet's message. After Brandish made it abundantly clear that he would not follow Franklin anywhere, he suddenly realized it left him no option but to return to The Great City. So he left discouraged and disgruntled."

"It sounds like he did go back to The Great City after becoming disillusioned by the words of the prophet."

"Yes, that is what he said, but his demeanor said otherwise. He was not at all looking forward to going back there. It would not surprise me if he spends some time in Wilderwood seeking out the scribe from Dogwood."

"Is there anything else you can tell me Beth?"

Beth suddenly recalled the flood of emotions she felt for the muscular blacksmith which swept over her that night. "No," she said abruptly.

Daria glanced down at Beth sitting in the uncomfortable straight back chair staring again at the curved stone wall of the tower. She did not appear to be the same girl when Daria left the manor. Daria was genuinely surprised and impressed by Beth's daring escape, her plan to work for the Duchess of Dogwood, and now she learned that the prophet had visited her shy quiet friend. *Her life has taken a turn down a different road, one she did not intend, and she fears she may not be able to return to the road she was on. She may be right.*

6

Closing In

W hile Franklin, John, and Luther lie in wait for Brandish at the end of Tenth Street, a small vessel that carried the emissary along with Kai, Baker, and Ursula docked along First Street. Thomas, one of Merrill's guards, noticed the emissary, and he summoned Merrill. The officer warmly greeted the emissary. "Who is she?" he asked gazing at the attractive blonde who was with the emissary's company.

Page sighed. "It is a long story, and we have nothing to show for our efforts except her. I did not see Driscoll the cook with Lady Kettery, but I am not concerned about him. His motivation for the journey was only to draw the boy back to The Corner Tavern. He was simply at the wrong place at the wrong time. Merrill, how have you fared?"

"Four prisoners, my lord, and one of them is Daria. We captured her and a friend who journeyed with her as soon as they arrived in port – late yesterday."

"Is the other girl Beth?"

"Yes."

"And the other two prisoners?" Page asked enthusiastically.

"Harbinger and Quayfear."

"Merrill!" Page said with a smile, "You have had a much more productive journey than we."

"Where is Ulric my lord?"

The emissary glanced at the others who remembered all too well the bloody fate of Ulric in the imaginary village of Pinewood, and answered quickly, "I left him in Dogwood to aid the Duke in temporarily running the fiefdom. I have obtained some useful information from the Duke of Dogwood. I will share that with you."

"The four prisoners are awaiting your arrival in Edgewood."

"Good, I will take Kai and Baker with me tomorrow at first light. I want your knights enquiring at every inn of the whereabouts of Franklin and the boy and Luther. They may be here in Wilderwood."

"We have spoken to the head of the guild here, and he will inform us if Luther shows up."

"Then Kingsley has aided you well?"

"He turned in our four prisoners."

"Ah! He wants knighthood badly."

"Apparently...though Kingsley said that he did not think he could identify the Baron. He only saw him briefly at the testing grounds and not up close."

"The Baron is deeply involved. Let us go to your room. We need to speak in private."

*

Merrill leaned forward on his chair listening as Page elaborated on his conversation with the Duke of Dogwood. He had told him everything except of the unexpected hamlet along the Southern Way. At its conclusion Page asked, "What do you make of it?"

"It sounds like the kings of the West are on the move."

"Kai suspects the same. I'm not so sure," Page said pensively.

Merrill sat still, noticing Page was deep in thought. Finally he asked, "Do you think the Fartherwoods killed the knights, my lord?"

"I don't know," Page said and leaned back in the chair. "What do you think?"

"Some of the men think you are blind to the obvious. Most believe the Fartherwoods killed them."

"I didn't ask about the other men, Merrill, I asked you."

"Perhaps the interrogations will shed more light on the issue."

"Yes, perhaps," said Page with a frustrated sigh, once again disappointed that his officer had no opinion on an important matter or was too afraid to give it.

The two men stepped outside and walked together down the road that hugged the River Green. The last ship of the day docked where the two men stood. It was Page who recognized Lady Kettery from Fartherwood, though he was not that surprised to see her again.

"My lady," he said as she debarked down the ramp of the ship and onto the dock followed by a young servant girl and Driscoll, who he was surprised to see. "I have good news. Daria and Beth have been captured by my knights here in Wilderwood. I will return your servant Ursula with, of course, some compensation for your trouble." He turned to his officer. "Merrill, get her."

Lady Kettery was aghast. She wanted Beth back – not Ursula. She saw the blonde servant walking towards her revealing no animosity or vengeance, though no doubt it was there hidden beneath a calm exterior. Lady Kettery smiled to herself. *Ursula gives nothing away. I have taught her well. I underestimated her tact and discipline.*

"Thank you for the loan of your servant for the good of the Realm, my lady," said Page.

"Since Daria has been caught, I assume you have no further need of Beth either," Lady Kettery said a matter-of-factly.

"If she had not escaped, she would be innocent of any transgression but as it is she must be interrogated as to her motive for escaping."

"She was merely trying to help her friend my lord. Her motive was pure, though misguided."

"If that is the case, she will be released after the interrogation – but not before," the emissary said finishing on a final note.

"Yes, my lord, you are most just and fair, goodnight."

"Goodnight, my lady."

"Come," she said to her servants in a restrained even tone. They followed her to a nearby inn.

*

That evening Brandish met Franklin, John, and Luther near the edge of the township with provisions and a small fishing net. "Let us be going," Franklin said, though not with his usual degree of confidence. He now realized after the incident at the pool in Candlewood around the statue of Wyeth the god of all waters that there was a power behind those lifeless entities. His special sword was mighty indeed for cutting anvils and through bones of deadly carnivores, but how would it fare against forces outside of his known world?

On the second floor of the Shady Inn the man known to Brandish as Sourlip the prophet's assistant leaned out the window and glanced up the road watching the four men leave Wilderwood. He spoke softly to himself, "Brandish has fallen for the lie that he was meant to be the proper vehicle for leading this crusade instead of Franklin. Brandish is too caught up in himself to see that Franklin is indeed the proper man to lead them. So as long as Brandish submits to Franklin's authority Franklin will not suspect anything, but there is no predicting how Brandish will behave. He may get too eager, push ahead with too much zeal, thus inclining Franklin to suspect foul play.

"Sometimes these creatures do things borne out of emotion or stupidity that are detrimental to their well-being – most peculiar. Yet, because of the White King's propensity towards mercy and forgiveness towards such weak and frail creatures, no move can be underestimated no matter how much folly it is conceived in."

The four men began their trek into the woods ahead. "My lord," asked John, "how long do you think it will take to get beyond Edgewood?"

Brandish interrupted, "I asked a shopkeeper that very question. I was told two days by foot or in our case two nights."

"It will be good to be beyond Castle Edgewood."

"As long as it is not too *far* beyond Edgewood," remarked Luther, "I just need to remain out of sight for a while until the guard give up this chase and return to The Great City."

"And I likewise," said Brandish, not desiring to give Franklin the notion that he was too eager to stay on.

*

The next morning the emissary along with Kai and Baker boarded a boat for Edgewood. Lady Kettery stood on the stoop outside the inn. She smiled and waved at the emissary indicating she would be right here waiting when he returned with Beth. Whatever happened to Daria was of no consequence to her.

After the emissary's departure, Merrill summoned his men and Kingsley to begin their search inn by inn for Franklin and the boy and Luther who never showed up at the guild. By midday the knights arrived at the Shady Inn. Two large maples like ancient sentinels stood outside the establishment, though today the sun shone brightly through the budding limbs.

Merrill, Thomas, Tobias, and Kingsley entered. Merrill's other men surrounded the sickly looking structure in case the fugitives tried to secretly leave out of a lesser known exit.

"My lords," said the owner with a glimmer in his eyes, "do you need some rooms?"

"No," said Merrill, "but information. We are looking for a young man traveling with a teenage boy – any such wayfarers?"

"The day before yesterday two young men with a teenage boy came to the inn to meet a guest named Brandish."

The innkeeper noticed Kingsley give a knowing glance to Merrill. Some intrigue was afoot he thought, and he was somehow caught up in it.

"Describe the other two men who traveled with the teenage boy," Merrill said to the owner.

They want information and information may lead to compensation. "One was short. He was the older one of the three – the other a tall lanky young man."

"That is no doubt Luther," said Kingsley.

Merrill turned to the proprietor. "And they left here two days ago?"

"Yes, but the odd thing is that they did not head towards the river, but they went up Tenth Street which terminates at the little used road to Edgewood, and I did not see them return. These men were far and away from being knights of the Realm, yet there is no other possible destination in that direction but the fortress."

Merrill placed four quib on the front counter.

The proprietor's eyes lit up. It paid off. He would be the talk amongst the innkeepers.

"Speak to no one about this. If you do, we'll be back, and it won't be a pleasant visit."

"Of course, my lord," the owner said, his face downcast, saddened because he could not boast of the money and how he was caught up in secret matters of the Realm.

Merrill and the others stepped outside.

When out of earshot, Kingsley spoke, "Brandish is Daria's brother, but he did not go with us into the wilderness, though he was there for the reading of the scroll. His plans were to go right back to The Great City."

"Mm, it seemed his plans had changed...why?" asked Merrill.

"Should we follow them?" questioned Thomas.

"No, they are unaware of our knowledge of their whereabouts. If we do not interfere, they will head right to the fortress. We will leave now for Edgewood by boat and inform Page on this latest development. He will decide what to do next."

Merrill turned to the young Fartherwood, "Everyone who left Fartherwood is now accounted for except the Baron. You have done well Kingsley."

The young man smiled. Knighthood was near.

The emissary along with Kai and Baker docked in the small hamlet outside of Edgewood. They traversed the gradual incline to the castle upon a hillock. Page spoke as they proceeded, "I will interrogate the four prisoners tomorrow."

"Perhaps this will solve some of the mystery," said Kai.

"Or add to it."

The following morning Harbinger was brought into a midsize sparsely furnished room with a small fire. As he stood amidst a palace guard and the knight from Dogwood and the emissary he noticed the exterior wall behind where the emissary sat covered with a large tapestry which held off some of the dampness emanating from the cold stone wall. Displayed upon the intricate weaving was a depiction of when the Barman's moved west across the Dark Mountains in their conquests. After being led into an ambush just outside of The Great City, they incurred great losses as the armies of the Realm descended upon them. Harbinger had heard the story often as a boy, but here it was displayed in picture form huge and colorful.

The emissary who had sat at ease now leaned forward resting his forearms on the table top before him. "Sit," Page said pointing to a vacant chair.

Page quickly began, "Let me get to the point Harbinger. You are accused of killing five of the Baron's knights in the wilderness. Yet you claim your innocence. Kingsley has made the accusation that the Baron killed his own men. We do have some serious issues with Durkel. For one thing he is missing, and he is in search of a scroll in Franklin's possession. These actions concern the Realm, but they alone do not directly tie him to this heinous act. But I am willing to listen to any credible motivation the Baron might have involving the death of those knights."

The emissary now leaned back in his chair and waited.

Harbinger sat before the emissary dumbfounded. What defense had he? Harbinger glanced at the two knights and behind them the tapestry. The picture on the hanging rug had changed. It now boasted a giant owl carrying a man. This man dangled helplessly from its talons staring down in utter fear at the vast wilderness below. That man was him! Harbinger was stunned, but he tried to hide any anxious movements and calmly faced the emissary, forcing his gaze away from the tapestry.

"You have nothing to say in your defense?" Page questioned becoming impatient at the stupefied pause. "Your life depends on it. If you can't convince me that the Baron could possibly be involved in the killings, then the blame will certainly fall on you and your group."

"The only thing I could say would only bring ridicule and laughter, and in the end I and the others would be found guilty anyway."

Page leaned forward again. "May I suggest, since your life is on the line, that you risk a little laughter at your expense. Who knows, it may save your life."

"I left Fartherwood only because Kingsley fell for the romance of this adventure hinted at in the scroll. I went along to convince him of his childish behavior – that knighthood awaited him and possibly duty as a palace guard. I succeeded in convincing him at the close of the first day."

Harbinger glanced again at the mural of the giant owl and himself dangling from it. He again faced the emissary and spoke, "That night I had a dream. In the dream I was delivered to the Baron by a giant owl. The Baron told me that he had joined an army more powerful than the Realm and that he saw potential leadership qualities in me at the testing grounds to aid them in their quest of The Midland Realm. Though there was one thing required of me and that was to kill Franklin and bring the scroll to him."

Here Harbinger paused and glanced around to catch what he assumed to be questionable expressions on their faces at such a puerile defense. Yet, surprisingly, the three others listened with interest.

He swallowed and continued. "I laughed at the notion that some great kingdom needed to employ me to kill Franklin, a mere scribe. The Baron reprimanded me for taking it so lightly. He repeated his command to kill Franklin, and then I woke up on watch where I had fallen asleep."

Harbinger's gaze followed the emissary's who looked at the other two knights and then back at him. No one was laughing.

Harbinger found the silence nerve racking. Finally the emissary spoke: "Interesting. Where is this kingdom the Baron spoke of? I know the more time has elapsed the more difficult it is to remember a dream."

"That is not the case with this dream. I can still clearly recall it as if it really happened. This kingdom is led not by a king but by a prince in Genadar."

At this last remark Harbinger saw that all three men became unsettled at the reference to this prince. *Such a man might exist.* Harbinger resumed his defense. "The next day I left with Kingsley, Luther, Driscoll, and Quayfear for Fartherwood, but we got lost and ended up back at our camp, which is where we found the dead knights. The next morning we started again for Fartherwood and arrived at dusk. The following day Quayfear and I left for Wilderwood."

"What is so special about Franklin that the Baron would want him killed?" Page asked.

"There seemed to be nothing special about him except his willingness to believe what was written in the scroll."

At this the emissary leaned forward again placing his hands flat on the table. "Is there anything else that you can add to your plea of innocence?"

Harbinger bowed his head slightly and shook it. "No, my lord," he said. Harbinger glanced back at the mural. The battle scene was again present.

Page turned to his guard and said, "Kai, take him back to his room and bring the scribe."

Page glanced at Baker after Kai escorted Harbinger out of the room. "Hold your thoughts until we've heard them all."

He nodded.

*

Quayfear sat in the vacant chair. He was close enough to the emissary to make him out clearly. The other two knights were a little blurry. The emissary asked Quayfear for a good reason to believe in his innocence and what motivation the Baron might have for killing his knights.

"The Baron is doing the bidding of another, it seems, and I believe his motives for the murders are related to that. A knight from outside of the Realm visited Durkel in Dogwood. His name is Sandgrit."

Although Quayfear could not see the other two knights in the room that well, he noticed them stir uneasily in their seats, and the emissary's fitful glance at the other two revealed his knowledge of this man. The emissary responded abruptly trying to smooth things over. "We know little of him. He is under suspicion. Perhaps you can fill us in."

Quayfear, who found the Baron frightening and intimidating, found the emissary's presence unthreatening and was somewhat relieved to pass this information on to some real authority. "The Baron has joined forces with whomever Sandgrit serves. It is Sandgrit's superior who wants the scroll and has given that task of finding it to the Baron. The one Sandgrit serves has a nemesis called the White King, who has a son whose name is Dresler. Sandgrit reported that Dresler was in the area disguised as a beggar. While in Fartherwood there was a vagrant loitering around the tavern. Franklin believed that he was Dresler and that he had placed the scroll there."

"So the scroll initiated from this White King was delivered by his son disguised as a pauper?"

"Yes, my lord, it appears that way."

"But who is this White King?"

"No one knows for sure…but he appears to be from the realm of the gods. I suspected this the from the first, since we overheard the Baron talking with Sandgrit, and our experiences thus far are confirming this to be the case, my lord."

"Very well, I will consider what you have told us, including this work carried out by beings in the spirit realm."

Quayfear was surprised and encouraged by the emissary's willingness to consider what he already was convinced of – that this was nothing less than the work of a god, perhaps a God above all gods.

Page turned his attention to Kai. "Bring Daria."

*

Daria sat down very lady-like and crossed her legs as if being interviewed for a position. Page thought she could easily pass as Lady Kettery's daughter, haughty and self-centered. "Is it true," Page began "that the only reason you left Fartherwood in search of Harbinger was because he was considering your hand in marriage?"

"That is true my lord."

"I see." He looked over at his knight. "Kai, bring me Beth."

"Wait," Daria said flabbergasted that the questioning ended so abruptly. "I demand to know what has happened to disrupt my life. Harbinger and I were to be married. He was to become a knight, possibly a palace guard!"

"You will know what has disrupted your life as soon as I know what has disrupted mine." He then gave a sideways nod to Kai, and she was removed from his presence.

*

Beth nervously looked around the room.

"You realize," the emissary stated, drawing her eyes to the desk where he sat, "that had you not escaped you would not be sitting here."

"Yes, my lord, it was a foolish thing to do. I just...I just..."

"You just what? Speak up."

"I just wanted to work for the Duchess of Dogwood."

Page nodded. "I don't blame you for wanting be rid of Lady Kettery but that was not the way to go about it."

"I wanted to be like Daria."

"And have you become like Daria?"

"No matter how hard I try or what I do, I will never be the bold untrammeled woman she is."

"So, what of it?" the emissary succinctly responded and turned towards his knight. "Kai lead her back to her room."

*

Kai reentered the room and shut the door and plunked himself down in the chair. "Well," he stated, "that was an earful...talking about Harbinger and Quayfear of course."

Page calmly leaned forward and addressed his knights, "It is clear to me that the Baron killed his knights. What is disturbing is that he is in cahoots with this Sandgrit character, whoever he may be who is under some prince in Genadar whoever he may be. Harbinger's dream coincides enough with Quayfear's story, and from what we've seen in Pinewood Harbinger's dream might have been more than just a dream."

"It seems these men happened to get caught up into something unawares," said Kai, "as we had. So what do we do now?"

"We will send Beth to Wilderwood tomorrow with some compensation for Lady Kettery for her trouble and to finally be rid of her. Quayfear is of value to us because he can identify the Baron. Harbinger may have experienced these supernatural powers of this prince as we have. I want him here. Daria is free to go if she chooses to, but she may stay here with Harbinger as long as she is no trouble. I will inform the commander of the keep of my decision."

"What have you to say about Quayfear's summation of the work of the gods?" asked Kai.

"There is plenty of evidence to conclude some involvement from the spiritual realm. It seems the key is the identity of this White King and his son Dresler."

Do gods have sons?" Kai inquired."

Page shrugged his shoulders.

"What is our next step, my lord?" Baker asked.

"Find Franklin before the Baron does."

"Do you think he can add any new information to what we already know?"

"There is only one thing he might be able to add. Why he is heading into the wilderness when an attack is planned on the city of Vale."

"A diversion perhaps?"

"Perhaps...or something else?"

*

The iron clad heavy oak gates were opened at this hour. Daria and Beth passed through with their escort and plodded down to the water's edge, practically dragging their feet as if the scuffing of them against the hard packed road might give them a little more time together. Though they spoke little, it was the physical comfort of a like companion in a strange environment that mattered most. They rounded a corner and Beth saw a boat waiting to take her to Wilderwood. She was told Lady Kettery was expecting her.

"No doubt a knight will deliver me to my lady's door," she remarked, breaking the silence which seemed difficult to shatter. "My fate has been sealed."

"If you were able to escape the emissary, you can escape the grasp of our lady and make your way to Dogwood…if you get the urge," Daria said and smiled.

Beth gave her a knowing smile back. "I have not ruled that out."

"What about you?" Beth asked her friend.

"Harbinger is released, though confined to the castle, which is a slight improvement of his status. Whatever happens, I won't be returning to the manor."

"I know. You were made for this adventurous life. Soon I'll be back at the manor, back in the routine."

The two girls hugged by the river and said their goodbyes again. The knight who had escorted them aided Beth into the boat. She sat near the front and faced upriver. Daria looked on until the boat neared a bend. Beth raised her arm and waved. Daria did likewise. Then Beth disappeared around the bend and was gone.

Daria turned and headed back up the incline gazing once again at the high walls. Unlike Dogwood and Driftwood, Edgewood was uninviting – resourceful yet utilitarian. It had little comfort, no beauty, and few luxuries; yet Daria felt safe and at the northern extremity of the Midland Realm that was most important.

8

Up the River Green

A t the end of the day a sudden knock startled the emissary who sat in his room. "Yes, come in," the emissary ordered.

"My lord, Merrill has arrived from Wilderwood," the courier announced and then departed.

"Any news on Franklin?" the emissary asked as Merrill entered and shut the door.

"Some good news concerning Franklin, at last, my lord: He, John, Luther, and another – the innkeeper said his name was Brandish, whom Kingsley informed us is Daria's brother left Wilderwood the night before last. They're coming this way and should be in the vicinity sometime this evening. With all the knights we have at our disposal in Edgewood we can thoroughly comb the woods around the castle. We'll find them my lord."

"Maybe, but if we don't they will backtrack and head south, and we will lose them again. No, it is better we let them pass the fortress unhindered. Once past Edgewood they will have to follow the riverbank or get hopelessly lost in the forest. We will wait and let them think they have gotten by us unnoticed. We can quickly catch up to them by boat."

"Did the interrogations reveal any new information?" Merrill asked.

"No, just more of what we had already learned in Dogwood. It is Franklin we need to hear from now."

"Understood, my lord."

"Good work, you are dismissed."

The Baron strode towards the window that faced the wilderness. *Franklin, Franklin, what is out there?*

*

The pale light of dawn now lit the way for Franklin, John, Luther, and Brandish as they trudged along the banks of the River Green having cleared the fortress by traveling undetected in the dark. Franklin said to the others, "We shall continue until noon and then sleep the rest of the day and through the night and resume a normal schedule in the morning."

No one argued. Traveling at night was painstakingly slow and frustrating. For Franklin it brought back memories of his friend Quayfear. How extremely difficult this trek would have been for him had he been here, yet what treatment was he receiving in the hands of the palace guard? Brandish had relieved his spirit some when he said Harbinger and Quayfear seemed to be in good physical condition when he had seen them from the window of his room at The Shady Inn.

At sunrise of the following day Franklin and his cohorts were well rested but hungry. The small fishing net was cast, garnering a few pickerel, boney but edible. During breakfast Luther spoke little.

Franklin noticed Luther's long face and was suddenly aware of his ongoing despondency and how unsympathetic he had been towards Luther's plight. His own association with Baron Durkel had become unbearable, and he had little to lose by leaving. Luther, however, had a bright future ahead of him. The woodworker had lost a lot, and Franklin had not been sensitive to Luther's situation.

Luther sat staring at the ground forlornly, his elbows resting on his knees with his chin couched in the cup of his hands. Franklin lightly nudged Luther with his foot. The woodworker looked up. "What?"

"I think," said Franklin, "that you should travel with us to the Plains of Lanashear. If there is nothing to this scroll and no one awaits us there, it is over. There should be some thriving communities which might be eager to welcome a woodworker like you. Because they are outside of the Realm you will not need any formal papers, just proof of your skills. In time this whole thing will be just a memory to the emissary, and it will be much safer for you to return."

Luther blinked in surprise, apparently pleased that Franklin for once had his interest at heart. He nodded slowly, mulling over what Franklin offered: a good and safe temporary resolve to his situation.

Franklin noticed for the first time since they had run into each other on the Northern Way a sense of relief and anticipation in Luther's expression. He now sat up straight and spoke, "I will do as you suggest. I will go to the plains."

"And what about you," Franklin asked addressing Brandish.

"As you suggested earlier after the palace guards interrogate the proprietor of The Shady Inn, they will likely conclude we left that night for Edgewood. Like Luther, I will go with you to the plains. I can work temporarily as a blacksmith if need be until I think it safe to return."

Franklin was silently relieved with their decisions to go on to the plains. He looked around at the tall pines which hugged the river's edge, some with large nests of sparrow hawks wedged among the upper branches and some shorter alders that grew along the banks swaying gently in a brisk spring breeze. He turned his attention downstream to a small shallow inlet where bulrushes grew. Northern bugle weed was plentiful as were different species of sedges.

Yet in spite of the beauty around them, there seemed an undercurrent beyond the possibility of a sudden appearance from the knights of Edgewood. Brandish and Luther looked unconcerned and unaware of the dread Franklin experienced, but he noticed fear and apprehension in John's demeanor. "What is it John?" Franklin asked.

"I have always dreamt of this day, a day of freedom from my father and Driscoll and The Corner Tavern, but I'd envisioned it with less of an anxious heart."

"Don't let your fears get the best of you John," Franklin said and abruptly ended this topic of conversation by standing to prepare for departure. *John senses what I have since we passed the fortress. I can see it in his eyes. He knows as I do there is something out here lurking, yet the other two are unaware of it. How does John know?*

Franklin's company covered more ground traveling by day, but still it was more tedious and difficult than Franklin had imagined. Some areas were soft and soggy exerting much energy to advance even a short distance and in others areas thickets of prickly bushes scratched and cut their flesh. They had finally come to a small dry clearing, and Franklin decided to camp there. No one argued.

*

Three sleek boats pushed away from the docks in Edgewood just prior to daybreak to find and apprehend the Fartherwoods upriver. Merrill along with three other palace guards were in the lead boat. The second boat which hung back a ways from the first one contained three more palace guards. The third boat manned by three more palace guards and Kingsley hung back a distance from the second boat. The oars broke the silence of the gray dawn as their blackened worn paddles sliced into the silvery current.

Towards the close of day Merrill gave the command to camp. The oarsmen guided the three boats towards the water's edge. The embankment was soft and mucky and would not be difficult for Ewar, an excellent tracker, to notice if the Fartherwoods had passed through.

Merrill glanced up at the dispiriting cloud cover which had descended upon the river. Beneath the dreary mantle the fading daylight was drab and listless. He had been sent on many a sortie before but never had he felt so disconsolate. Was it this place…or something else?

"Over here," said Tobias, "tracks….many!"

"How long ago?" Merrill asked Ewar.

"One to two hours…possibly three - four men."

"Tobias," Merrill ordered, "takes the last watch and wakes us up as soon as there is enough light to travel."

"We can paddle upriver in the dark," suggested Thomas.

"Yes, but we can paddle right by them, and lose them. We want to keep them from backtracking south."

*

Franklin awoke early. It felt like rain. "Get up," he said to the others. They stirred slowly. "We'll eat later. I want to leave now!"

They traveled for about an hour and had come to the bottom of a long set of wild rapids, and the noise of the racing water was nearly ear shattering in the quiet wood.

Franklin spoke loudly, "These rapids are the best thing that could have happened to us. If the guards travel by boat, they will have to abandon them here. They can go no farther. If Quayfear were here, he would say the gods have been good to us."

John toned in, "And I would say, Quayfear, you are right."

"Well, perhaps not that good," said Luther glancing up. "I felt a drop of rain."

Franklin responded, his face set firmly upriver, "No matter, we keep going."

They traveled a while with no end to the rushing rapids. A light rain was coming down now. Up ahead a giant white pine had recently fallen across the river, its needles still green.

Franklin thought he heard voices over the echoing rushing water. He turned and saw the knights. "They're here!" Franklin cried out. The others glanced behind. "Come!" Franklin called to his men and rushed towards the felled tree. He hopped onto the end of the pine which bridged the mighty river.

Franklin led the way through the thick prickly branches at the end of the tree. There was an abandoned hawk's nest amidst the entanglement. When Franklin cleared the limbs, the rest of the trunk was bare of branches save for a few stubby dead ones; so with arms outstretched for balance Franklin made his way to the end of the trunk that continued another ten feet or so into the wood beyond the banking.

John quickly followed closely behind Franklin. He was small and agile and had no trouble maneuvering through the web of branches and then down the massive trunk. He hopped off when he reached the other side.

Brandish was not so graceful but managed to muddle his way without mishap down the large trunk which hung just a few feet over the raging water.

Luther hurried through the mess of limbs but when he came to the open trunk, he hesitated; yet he was encouraged as he looked down its length and saw the girth increase with each step. Luther started slowly across the bare thick trunk.

"Hurry!" John cried.

In a panic Luther glanced backwards to see the location of the knights and lost his balance. He let out a screech and fell into the cold quick current.

"Luther!" John yelled in dismay.

Luther struggled with each breath in the fast bone-chilling water. The knights seemed an elusive blur as the mighty river pushed him down the rapids. A series of large rocks poked above the surface. He glided passed a couple ominous boulders and soon came to a slightly calmer section that increased in fury farther down. Luther noticed a large rectangle rock off to his left. If he did not find safety atop that stone, he would not survive the rapids below. Luther flailed his arms and legs wildly. As he passed by it he reached out and grabbed onto a small crag. He tried pulling himself out but was losing his grip.

Luther suddenly heard a voice over the raging river, though whether real or imagined he could only guess: *The sword – it's weighing you down. Get rid of it.*

Responding to the idea, he thought: *How shall I survive in the wilderness without it?*

What good is a sword on a drowned man's body? Save yourself.

The logic seemed clear. *Yes, I must unbuckle my sword.*

Luther let go with his left arm to reach for his belt. The current tore him from the boulder. He screamed as he slipped down into the swift passing water that engulfed him in a liquid funnel. It twisted and twirled his body like a rag below the surface. His battered frame hit another rock, and he barely managed to bring himself up. He gagged on some water, spitting out what he could while frantically trying to climb atop another stony island.

"*Let go,*" whispered the voice as smooth and powerful as the river itself.

Luther's response was feeble though determined: *No, not this time.*

His arms strained against the slippery water which was slowly peeling him off the rock. With his head just above the surface an eerie darkness closed in around him.

Then that voice returned. "*It is over now.*"

With a sudden surge the icy water pressed against Luther's body. He wrestled against the desire to simply let go and with his last bit of strength tried one more time to pull himself out, but the current was now more than he could bear.

*

Brandish gazed across the river as the knights neared the pine bridge. He saw Merrill point, and two of his knights started downriver to follow the woodworker after he raced by them in the icy water. The commander led the others towards the felled tree.

"My lord, what are we going to do about Luther?" John asked in a panic.

"Nothing now," interjected Brandish. "We've got to get away from the knights. They're nearly upon us."

"We cannot outrun them," Franklin said.

"We can hide deep in the woods, my lord, until the knights pass" John advised, "and then look for Luther."

"We may get hopelessly lost and never find our way back to the river. There is only one reasonable alternative," Franklin stated succinctly and pulled out his sword.

"We're going to fight them!" declared Brandish with a note of absurdity to his tone.

Franklin did not reply but swung at the thick trunk which cut through the wood fibers as if he were slicing cheese. The huge girth splashed into the river. Merrill jumped back onto solid ground on the opposite bank just as the raging river pulled the top branches into the river and with a terrible force sent it downstream. The palace guard stood dumbfounded, numbly staring at the tree shooting down the rapids.

Brandish spoke as if in a mesmerized state, "It really did split the anvil."

"Yes," said Franklin. "Now let's find Luther."

*

Ewar and Tybalt, who had hurried downriver to determine the woodworker's condition, now looked aghast as the large pine passed by them pushed along by the thundering rapids. They stopped in their tracks and stared in awe at the bizarre scene.

"What has happened up there?" questioned Tybalt, shouting above the turbulent river.

"We better start back! Besides, the rapids only worsen! I hold out little hope for that man's survival!"

"I concur!"

*

Luther found himself on top of the rock, though he had no recollection of the final moments. Gasping for air he looked upstream for any sign of the knights. He saw no one. The light raindrops were now coming down harder. Luther knew it was only a matter of time before the knights would find him perched on this rock in the river. But instead of the knights coming downriver he saw a huge pine tree hurling at him like an arrow. A cross current pushed it toward the opposing side they had traversed, and the bole of the great pine buried itself onto the embankment. The top of the evergreen fish tailed; and the web of branches came across the boulder and knocked Luther out cold, tangling his body in the midst of needles and pine cones and an abandoned hawk's nest. The larger limbs held the tree just above the rapids.

A squatty bald middle age fellow along the banking raised his head and cursed the White King for interfering. *Luther was as good as dead...but they'll be other chances.* He smiled wickedly. *There are forces out here much stronger and more frightening than the waters of the Green.*

Franklin held his company back from the river. They saw Ewar and Tybalt give up their search for Luther. They understood why.

"Is he dead my lord?" asked John, his voice stuttering in disbelief.

"Perhaps," Franklin answered.

"What do you mean perhaps?" Brandish flared. "You need to tell the boy the truth."

"Until we find his body his fate is uncertain."

"It obviously has been carried downstream. I suggest we don't waste any valuable time searching for Luther. The knights may find another way of crossing farther upstream."

Franklin looked sadly at John. "Unfortunately, Brandish is right. We must keep going. If Luther is alive, he must fend for himself now. It is a tough decision, and one I don't like making, but we must move on"

"I understand my lord," said John and said no more about it.

Franklin led his party upriver but kept far enough back, so they could not be seen. "Thanks to your sword once again we are saved," said John. He glanced over at Brandish. "This magic sword has saved us more than once."

"I wish I had a sword," said Brandish. "I feel helpless without one."

"You would be helpless with one," John responded. "I have a sword, and it has been no use thus far. It is Franklin's special sword that has kept us alive till now."

"That is true," Franklin conceded, "but I would not be able to fend them all off in a direct confrontation. We must keep ahead of them."

*

The rain had let up. "Let us camp here tonight," ordered Merrill. "We will continue our journey in the morning. Eventually a means will open for us to cross the river. But now to the important issue: Kingsley," Merrill stated firmly, "tell us all you know about that sword!"

"Yes, my lord." Kingsley began when Franklin split the anvil until his parting from Franklin early on in the wilderness.

"I don't believe in magic," said Merrill, "yet no sword no matter how sharp could slice through a thick pine. Even a sharp ax takes many swings." Merrill sat staring at the campfire Ewar had started. "Page was right. This affair seems to grow in strangeness."

9
Another Cog in the Wheel

The next morning the sky was clear and bright over the River Green. A constant roar rang in Luther's ears. He snapped open his eyes and saw a surging river only inches below his face. He found himself wedged tight at the hip between two branches. He tried twisting and wiggling to free himself, but he could not budge.

Suddenly a loud splitting groan came from the tree shifting in the soft riverbed as it slowly rolled and dropped several inches. Luther's left side was now submerged in the freezing cold water. It nearly took his breath away, but the shifting of the limb caused it to spread apart enough to loosen its vice-grip hold upon Luther's hip. He pushed himself up as hard as he could to free himself. Pain seared across his thigh as sharp edges of bark ripped portions of his trousers, scraping off bits of flesh. Luther winced in pain, but the freedom from his imprisonment was exhilarating. He crawled on hands and knees until he reached the edge of the river and rolled off the meaty trunk onto the embankment, shivering in the cool morning air.

The sudden relief of being on solid ground gave way to hysterical laughter which soon turned into uncontrollable crying. The shock of nearly drowning slowly wore off and was replaced by sudden anxiety. Where were the others? Had they assumed he died in the rapids and had given up the search, or were they themselves caught or killed by the knights? Suddenly a more immediate question arose: Whose melodious voice now carried over the swift moving waters rushing against rock and stone? Luther recognized the tune. It was a song the old men sang occasionally in the tavern.

Luther crept through the dense greenery until he spotted the mysterious minstrel pulling in a large bass from the river. He was an older man, short but pleasant in appearance. He had a band of hair below a bald scalp, and sported a cropped white beard. A robe-like smock was tied around his waist. He looked amicable enough. Luther couldn't tell for sure, but he did not notice a weapon. Still it was best to play it safe. He shouted from a distance, "Hello, I'm hurt and I'm lost."

The stranger grabbed his catch and ran into the woods.

"Stop," Luther hollered, "please come back!"

The hermit did not return. Luther went looking for him. "Ouch," he cried and winced at the pain from his bruised hip. He snapped a long dead branch to a comfortable size and used it to lean on. Luther walked a short ways but then hesitated. He could barely hear the river. At least he could still follow it south to Fartherland. If he continued away from the river, he was sure to get completely lost.

The security of the echoing rapids was calling him. Even now he found himself wrestling with the mighty Green. He listened to the swift waters glide around the impending rocks, and the rhythm of its steady flow beckoned him back; but he could not survive the long trek home without food and shelter, not to mention the unknown whereabouts of the palace guard. Determined to pursue the old loner, Luther planted his walking stick in front of him and tore himself away from the sounds of the commanding river. Soon all was silent except for his loud traipsing through the quiet forest.

He plodded along for some time. To his delight the woods were thinning out. The pines here were much older, four to six feet in diameter. Their roots protruded above the soil like long crooked fingers grasping the earth to keep them from toppling over. Their thick bark resembled an old overcoat that protected these masters from disease and decay. Luther heard the soft crunching of pine needles beneath his feet as he gazed up through the towering branches. Taking in the splendor of this place, it was only by chance that Luther's eye caught a glimpse of the recluse peeking around a gnarly tree.

"Don't run away," Luther pleaded. "I'm lost, and I can't go much farther alone."

"It is rare I see anyone this far upriver," said the hermit. "I don't like being surprised."

"I tried not to frighten you. My name is Luther."

"I am Brainwart," he said, coming out from his hiding and took in the sight of this rag-torn looking young man. "It looks like you fell into the rapids. It is a miracle you are alive! I live not far from here." The bearded hermit glanced up through the trees. "It will be dark soon. You are welcome to stay the night."

"Thank you, my good sir. I am in your debt."

The two men walked amongst the thick wooden pillars of this verdant palace. The land ascended swiftly and proved an arduous walk for Luther. Brainwart led them toward a bubbling stream. The waters cascaded over outcrops of rock forming a series of beautiful waterfalls. The clear water sparkled in the sunlight as it sprayed them when they walked by, and the sound of it deafened their voices and footsteps. Just ahead was a foot bridge, and beyond that Luther noticed a small cabin nestled among the ancient trees.

The cabin was square with a small rectangle wing off the back. The windows and doors were arched, unlike the sharp hard angles in the architecture of Fartherwood. The rustic dwelling was weathered but tidy. Inside the interior wood was smooth, and the edges of exposed timbers were rounded to soften their bulky appearance. There was a loft above for guests similar to Luther: nomads, strays, fugitives, and the like. In the center of the room was a large hearth for cooking. Brainwart pointed to a small stack of kindling. "Start a fire Luther. I'll gut the fish."

Luther was excited about sleeping under a roof and drying his wet clothes. He lit the fire and sat in a large comfortable chair not far from the warm stone oven. He sighed with relief. Brainwart came out with the fish in an iron skillet. "Is there

anything I can do?" Luther asked wondering if he would even
be able to lift himself out of the chair

"No, just relax. Tell me about how you came to be so far up
the River Green."

Luther saw no point in telling him the complicated truth. "A
friend of mine and I went hunting for game in the wilderness.
When he hadn't returned to our bivouac, I went looking for him.
The next thing I knew I also was lost. I finally made my way to
the river. I was walking too close to the embankment along the
rapids, tripped and fell in and now here I am."

Luther, desiring to change the subject, glanced around at the
fine workmanship inside the cabin. "You seem to know a little
bit about wood."

"I am a wood wright from the town of Seven in the province
of Glendyland. At one time a bright future lay before me,
but rumors of a buildup of Barman forces beyond the Dark
Mountains spread. According to the soothsayers, our gods
prophesied of peace, so the king put off preparing a defense until
the last minute.

"Young and eager for adventure I set down my tools and
picked up a sword. I marched with the knights boasting of a
quick victory. Many commoners fought and died alongside the
knights. In a desperate situation I fled. In my shame I followed
the River Green north and settled here. I thought to go back
someday, yet the more I planned on doing so, the longer I put it
off."

Luther then noticed Brainwart looking far off in thought.
"What are you thinking?"

"I have wasted my life in the wilderness." He then stared
blankly beyond Luther.

"I too am a woodworker," Luther said to break the awkward
silence. "I have just finished my apprenticeship."

Brainwart cheered up. "It is good to have a visitor I have
something in common with. I'll cook the fish." The two men
enjoyed the bass sprinkled with herbs. The topic of conversation

changed, and the Barman crossing was not brought up again. It wasn't long before Luther started to doze in the comfortable chair.

*

"It is the end of the second day and no sign of them," said one of the palace guards who wearily trudged along while glancing fitfully across the wide river for a glimpse of the runaways from Fartherwood.

"They're there," Merrill said. "They are holding themselves back from the water's edge so we can't see them, hoping we will give up and think they've backtracked, but they have revealed nothing but determination to get this far. I am not convinced they will turn around."

"I suppose."

"Up ahead...look!" said a guard who had taken the lead, "A ford!"

"Excellent," said Merrill, "and no doubt we have gotten here first. They would not have made as good time keeping back from the river. We'll set up camp on this side. I don't want us taken by surprise during the night with that magical sword on the loose. I want two knights on guard per watch. Tomorrow we will cross the ford and spread out a ways from the river's embankment forming a human net. They cannot help but run into us."

*

The shutters of Brainwart's cabin were closed. The night air was cool and the forest exceptionally quiet. A tremor passed under the floorboards and shook the small house. It woke Luther from a deep sleep. "What was that?" he asked.

"I don't know," Brainwart said cautiously looking for damage. Seeing none, his rotund frame circled the room picking up knick-knacks, cooking utensils, and some pans that were shaken off their pegs.

And again the furnishings rattled as a quick shudder ran through the cabin – then it stopped. Brainwart ran out to the porch while Luther went to get his sword. As Brainwart's eyes adjusted to the darkness he saw a giant lizard-like animal standing upright at the edge of the clearing, blacker than the night around it. Leathery wings were folded tight against hard scalloped plates, and its hind feet were long and heavy looking. The creature's breathing was onerous, emanating a foul smell. A white vapor came from two large nostrils at the end of an elongated snout.

Without saying a word Brainwart dashed toward the pines and vanished into the woods.

Luther ran onto the porch, but the old man was gone. "Where are you?" he called.

The tall creature fell forward on all four legs bringing its massive head only a few feet from its puny adversary. Its jaundice colored eyes glared at him. Luther felt himself being sucked into a kind of vortex. With his last ounce of strength he tore himself from the glare, turned, and hobbled back into the little house and through the workshop. The enormous foot of the monster came crashing down upon the roof.

The rafters caved in just as Luther ran out the back door. The ground shook as the thundering beast stomped hard upon the cabin. Small nocturnal animals nearby stopped in their tracks and quickly turned their heads towards the sounds of rampage and scurried to their forest dwellings.

Luther could hear sharp snaps of timbers fracturing behind him as he fled. Grinding sounds of board against board shattered the dark stillness of the quiet woods. The forest itself, only a short distance from the clearing, appeared to jettison backwards as he drew near it. Luther furtively extended his arms reaching out to clutch the trees and draw them to himself.

In a few moments he found himself within the safety of the wood and realized the delusion was brought upon by the dragon. He noticed a wide stubby tree which over the years, through rot and decay, had hollowed out a large upright crevice. He squeezed inside the dank cavity which faced the oncoming beast. Luther shuddered as the sounds of the crashing feet drew near. Small chips of soft rotten wood crawling with insects shook loose upon the frightened man.

The black thing plodded towards the tree. Then that same voice he heard while in the river, whispered – *"Run! It is not safe here."* At that the towering structure stopped and a sudden silence filled the air. Luther looked down and saw a black leathery foot very near. Although the creature's large head was high above and could not possibly see him, Luther felt exposed. Every urge, every fiber of his body commanded him to leave the safety of the confining rot of the decaying tree. He fought against this pull that threatened to draw him out into the open.

He shut his eyes and remained still and casting off that whispering voice he stood motionless within the dirty crumbling rot around him. Time seemed suspended as both sides waited out the other in a battle of nerves.

Moments later Luther heard some limbs directly above snap and fall to the ground. The dire monstrosity pressed on. Luther relaxed a little as the prodigious footsteps of the reptile became faint as it made its way toward the river. The wood wright from Fartherwood stepped out from the hollow of the dead tree and brushed his clothes off, astounded after his fall into the river and this attack from a dragon that he was still alive, but he was, save for a bruised hip and a temporary limp.

Luther gazed at the clearing, overwhelmed by the abrupt termination of a man's abode once filled with character and charm – in moments wiped away. Luther could do nothing but stare at the heavy timbers split asunder crisscrossing each other in heaps upon the broken floor. His head turned at the groaning sound of a lone teetering wall, as if struggling to maintain its precarious balance.

Luther looked for Brainwart but could not find him, leaving him to conclude that the old hermit was eaten by the filthy beast.

He tried not to dwell on the poor man's fate. Just then he heard a noise in the woods close to where he stood. He made out a man walking towards him. "Brainwart," Luther cried out, "you're alive!"

"Luther, you escaped that thing," Brainwart responded in glee. After the two men rejoiced to see each other, Luther said, "Why didn't you tell me such a beast lived out here in the wilderness?"

"I have been out here for three decades and have never seen anything like that. Although I have heard tales of dragons, I never gave them much credence. That beast matched descriptions I had heard from those whom I thought were dotty folks... madding types who spent too much time with witches and their concocted brews."

Luther glanced at the wreckage and sensed that this was his doing, that his presence here lured this beast from out of its distant lair. "I have not been honest with you," Luther began.

"You mean you're not a wood wright."

"No, that part is true. It is how I came to be out here. It is a long tale."

"Are you under some kind of curse by the gods, banished from Fartherland?"

"I don't know exactly what is happening to me. Let me tell you my story and you judge."

Luther, who thrived on spinning yarns at the tavern, was in his element here and began with the first night in The Corner Tavern. "It began," he started, "when John, a boy who helped at the tavern, found this scroll..."

At the conclusion of Luther's account Brainwart glanced at Luther's sword, realizing that the wood wright was leaning towards belief in what Franklin had been telling him. Brainwart then spoke in order to eradicate that thought, "I am glad you remained hidden and did not attempt to take on that creature yourself. There are no such thing as magical swords."

"I know!" Luther snapped defensively.

"Your friend Franklin is a fool."

That was exactly how he had perceived Franklin…until now. He glanced down at his sword and thought of that commanding voice he heard at the river to let go of his sword lest he drown – and again here in the crevice of that rotting tree that same voice tempting to lure him outside of safety, exposing him to the dragon. *John was right: Banebreath, the wolves, and now this creature. They are all in cahoots. I know this now. I don't know how and why I now know this – I just do.*

Brainwart softened his speech. "I will admit this Franklin sounds a little strange, and it was not my intention to speak poorly of your friend. I'm sure he means well."

*

John cocked his head instantly waking from a deep sleep when he heard a distant roar…then nothing. *Thunder?* John lay back exhausted and was asleep before his head hit the ground.

Four leagues upriver the two knights on watch had heard it too. They concurred with each other. The noise was not imagined but its source was impossible to determine. It was decided that they would alert the others if they heard it again. They did not.

The knights on watch were tense as the evening wore on from being on extra alert since hearing the strange noise. A loud thump broke the strained atmosphere - then another. The two knights glanced around, their swords drawn…then quiet - nothing. "What do you think?" asked Peyton whispering to Gavin.

"Probably a large bear on the other side - any sound in this quiet wood at night is magnified greatly."

They were reluctant to wake those sleeping. Except for the gurgling sounds of the current running over the stony bottom of the shallow ford, the forest was deathly quiet. "Something is wrong," said Peyton softly. He separated from the other sentry and slowly walked downstream where the sounds of the bear or whatever it was had emanated from.

Gavin saw a streak of yellow flame course across the River Green alighting on Peyton. "Aiee!" he screeched.

The other knights awoke startled. Kai grabbed his sword and hid in a thicket of brush when he heard the screeching voice of a tortured man. Gavin tried to douse the fire by rolling his friend in the shallow waters of the ford.

Kai heard some rustling from behind and saw Merrill yank Kingsley and Ewar towards the shelter of the dark wood. Kai remained where he was out of sight in the low brush cover, mesmerized by the brutal attack.

Thomas noticed the source of this fire coming from across the river, an immense creature barely distinguishable from the darkness around it. It was motionless, resembling a statue set up by some long forgotten people centuries before.

"Dragon!" Thomas hollered. Then with one quick movement the still beast cocked its head towards the sound of the knight's voice. Thomas, petrified by fear, dropped his sword and stood as if naked, exposed and helpless. A burst of fire shot across the ford and Thomas, like a human torch, lit up the night. And again the agonizing cry of horrific shrieks of unbearable pain reverberated in Kai's ears.

He looked on stunned, unable to move as the black statuesque savagery suddenly burst forth across the ford, its scaly plates like a moving fortress plowed toward his tiny sanctuary in the dense brush. Tobias' back faced Kai and the dragon's left foot smashed into the brave palace guard who stood unnerved in the shallows, his sword drawn. The sudden impact killed him instantly. Kai saw the limp body sail over his head and vanish into the woods.

He then saw another guard using stealth-like techniques to flank the creature. The man let loose an arrow, but it bounced off the hard plates. Kai wanted to scream '*Watch out!*' but for fear of his own life remained quiet as the dragon's long tail swung around smashing the knight's bones and sending the corpse through the air. Kai heard the body make sudden impact against a tree.

Gavin, who had been rolling Peyton in the shallow water, saw little hope for his charred and unconscious friend. He now remained still hoping the dragon would not see him. The creature halted in midstream sniffing the air.

The frightened knight in error made a dash to the safety of the trees when he felt a rush of heat against his back and unspeakable pain course over his flesh. He fell forward screaming in agony. His last sight on earth was Kai, a fellow palace guard, cowering in the bushes nearby. Kai turned his face away from the rage in his friend's eyes before they closed and he was no more.

Kai's attention shifted to the two remaining knights glancing frantically around for a way out. One of the men looked up and saw an open jaw drop quickly. The knight screamed as he breathed in the vile smell of the monsters breath as total blackness encapsulated him in the mouth of the dragon. The sharp teeth of the monster snapped him in half. The dragon raised its head chewing the upper body of the man. Kai stared blankly at the bottom half of his friend which collapsed in the water.

The beast lifted its massive leg. Tybalt had only enough time to glance up at the leathery pad of the giant foot as it came crashing down on him. He felt his insides compressed and then squeezed out of his body. It was quickly over.

Kai was an easy target if it could sense his presence. The foul thing raised its snout and sniffed but a light breeze blew upriver carrying Kai's scent away from the huge reptile. The great beast then looked down at the reddish water that flowed around the hulking feet, and let out a roar of victory. It turned and headed back from whence it came.

*

The Fartherwoods had awoken the instant they heard the roars of a beast and the cries of men in anguish.

"The knights are being attacked," Franklin said, "upriver!"

"By what?" questioned the boy? "What could it possibly be?"

"I don't know. Come!"

The three men made their way towards the water's edge.

"Did that creature pick up their scent?" the boy asked alarmed. "Could it find us?"

Franklin turned and spoke, "Whether the beast can pick up our scent or not, I cannot say, but we cannot do anything in the dead of night. The river may be our only means of escape if need be, so we should stay close to it."

No one could sleep. They sat quietly in the darkness fearing the worst.

A short time passed. All was quiet. Brandish laid his head down. He heard the ground vibrate. His eyes flashed open. "It's near!" he whispered frantically. Franklin slid out his sword.

At the sound of Brandish's words the creature broke into a run bending over large trees in its path, their massive root systems violently torn up, tossing huge clumps of sod into the air. Before the men had a chance to respond, the cruel creature had them hemmed in against the river's edge.

John ran along the embankment to escape but lost his balance and fell in the fast current which carried him quickly downriver. The dragon caught a glimpse of the young boy and shot a burst of fire at him, hitting the water but missing John who was swiftly carried out of range.

The dragon glanced around in the darkness looking for the others. Unable to detect them he shot a ball of fire upon a tall tree which burst into flames lighting up the dark night. Out of the corner of its eye it caught a glimpse of a short man raising his sword just above the trunk of its tail and down it came slicing the long heavy tail from the dragon's torso. The giant reptile let out a great moan of agony.

With the weight of its tail now cut off from the rest of its body the top heavy creature could not maintain its balance and fell forward into the cold deep waters of the river. The dragon's shorter front legs could not touch the bottom of the riverbed to push it up on its hind legs. The beast tried to keep its long snout above the surface but without the use of its tail and the strength it provided to maneuver its cumbersome body, the dragon raised its head one last time above the surface for a last gasp of air before going under.

The burning tree allowed the men to see a portion of the dragon humped above the surface of the water, its long tail separated from it and lying on the embankment of the river.

Franklin wasted no time going downriver a short ways looking for John, but he could not go far beyond the light of the flaming tree without stumbling beyond hope.

Brandish spoke over the crackling fire. "We will search for him in the morning."

Franklin nodded solemnly.

The water was icy cold. John grew weaker as he struggled to keep his head above the current. Just as it seemed all was lost John felt something hard floating near him – a tree broken asunder by the dragon. John grabbed a hold of it and managed to climb on. It caroused down the middle of the river. There was no way John could direct its course. He wondered how far it would carry him from the others?

Merrill, Kai, Ewar, and Kingsley heard the roar of the dragon downriver from them. "It has found the Fartherwoods," Merrill said. "I wonder if they fared any better than us."

"They have the special sword," Kingsley remarked.

"But could Franklin get close enough to use it?" Ewar questioned.

"Tomorrow we shall see," Merrill said.

*

Luther and Brainwart heard the distant roars of the beast at two distinct intervals. "It seems," surmised Brainwart, "that the beast attacked both your party and the knights. If they stood their ground against the creature, it is not likely that anyone survived."

"Our survival was not likely, but we're still here. Maybe they are too," Luther responded hopefully with masked uncertainty.

"In the morning we shall make our way to the river and see if we can find anyone alive."

10
Strange Bedfellows

John had all he could do just to hold on to the top half of a tree that had once stood proudly near the embankment before the reckless creature snapped it from its trunk. Now it surged downriver. John's wet legs and arms went numb in the frigid air. His right cheek lay against the wet cold bark while his teeth chattered. He hoped by now the current would have driven the tree onto one of the embankments, but the current kept it running down the middle. About an hour had passed when the dark sky above began to give way to a new morning. How far had he gone? The rapids lay ahead.

Suddenly John felt the tree nudge over to his right. He thought he might have hit a submerged rock close to the surface but moments later the log nudged over some more…and again, each time bringing him closer to the embankment until finally it careened into some low grasses which opened into a marshy area.

John rolled off the slippery wet bark. He tried standing in the murky bottom but his muscles were cramped from the cold. He crawled on his knees to solid ground and collapsed exhausted and shivering and covered in mud. He knew his survival depended on him staving off the cold. John had watched how nimble Luther was in making a fire from a wooden spindle and a piece of wood with a groove. With some effort John managed it and soon had a good blaze going. He laid his drenched body close to it and fell asleep.

*

"We have spent enough time searching for John," conceded Franklin while standing on the East bank of the River Green.

Neither the bright songs of a red-winged blackbird, nor the noisy caws of a blue jay were brightening Franklin's morning.

"Since he didn't fall into a set of rapids," remarked Brandish, "there is more hope of his survival than Luther's. This wilderness is no place for a boy anyway."

Franklin looked around at the endless forest that encompassed them. He was weary, saddened, and hungry. "It's no place for any of us," Franklin said despondently, "yet here we are and now just the two of us."

"Not just two," Brandish whispered urgently, "voices... down!"

Franklin slid out his sword.

Brandish pulled a couple of branches away and looked towards the sounds of crunching footsteps. "I don't believe it," said Brandish. "It's Luther and some old hermit."

Franklin stood up exuberant. "Over here!" he called.

"They're alive!" Luther shouted to Brainwart. Luther ran ahead of his new friend and the three embraced and rejoiced in their unexpected reunion.

"We want to hear all about your ordeal Luther," said Franklin, "but first who is this man? Did he rescue you?"

"He did indeed. His name is Brainwart."

Introductions were made. It was then that Luther asked, "Wait, where's John?" He noticed Franklin's countenance change immediately. "He fell into the river as yourself, but now seeing you alive, it has increased my hope for my friend. Now please tell us how you managed to survive the rapids."

Luther in his usual flair for storytelling made the attack of the dragon upon Brainwart's humble abode come to life. Franklin quickly filled them in on the roar of the beast upriver and the mayhem which must have followed and of the dragon's foray into their bivouac, though more as a list of facts than a drama of unbelievable proportion.

Afterwards, Franklin addressed Brainwart. "Do you know the quickest way to the Plains of Lanashear?"

"You must cross the river at the ford and travel upriver six days until you come to a trail that cuts through the remainder of the wilderness and from there a day's journey to the plains."

"We're not sure if some knights might have escaped the dragon's assault upon their camp," Franklin said. "We will proceed with caution."

"What about Brainwart?" Luther questioned. "The dragon destroyed his cabin. He saved my life. Let us welcome him into the company. He, too, is a wood wright. He and I can find work together somewhere on the plains."

"Of course, Brainwart, you may join us. Your knowledge of the wilderness will, I'm sure, prove invaluable."

Luther noticed Franklin cast one last glance downriver, hoping beyond hope that he might spy John washed along the riverbank. Then he turned and without a word started upriver towards the ford.

*

The new morning was without cheer. Merrill stood in a melancholic state upon the banks of the ford. He was responsible for bringing these drifters in, but instead had lost seven exemplary palace guards to a fire-breathing beast.

"This beast attacked the Fartherwoods shortly after its foray upon us," Ewar said. "Maybe they're all dead, and our duty here is over."

"Our duty here is over, regardless," said Merrill. "The Fartherwoods are not running from us. They're running from something else. We will go back after we bury our dead…or what is left of them."

The knights set to the grim task. After completing their duty, Merrill led his two remaining knights, Kai and Ewar along with Kingsley downriver. By midmorning Ewar stopped in his tracks when he saw a scaly hump protruding out of the water and cried out, "Look, in the river…the beast! And its tail rests upon the opposite shore!"

"It is the sword," exclaimed Merrill.

"Where did you get such a sword?" Ewar asked, addressing Kingsley. "You want to prove your knighthood. Here is your chance. What empowers that sword?"

"I do not know."

"You better have an answer before we get back to Edgewood. Ten palace guards leave Edgewood and seven are killed by a fire-breathing dragon. Yet the beast is slain by a scribe, a blacksmith, a wood wright and a boy? Page is going to want to know how this could be, and if you cannot answer, your chances of knighthood will vanish!"

"We've got more pressing matters than Kingsley's knighthood," Merrill stated in an apprehensive tone as his eyes slowly scanned their surroundings. "That creature might have a mate, so stay alert."

*

When John opened his eyes, the sun was high, but the fire was burning down. Across from the dying flames John saw a pile of bass with a small lizard-like creature curled up next to the fish sleeping comfortably.

John instinctively wanted to reach for his sword, but he was lying on it. He quickly jerked himself up and grabbed the hilt. The lizard immediately awoke and scampered a short distance away and then stopped.

John's clothes had dried out a bit, but they were still damp. He built up the fire and gutted the fish that the lizard had caught. The creature remained a safe distance away but did not leave. John noticed it had to be about three to four feet in length. He then realized it was this creature which had butted the log towards the shore. It had saved his life and even caught fish for him to eat.

The longer he looked at the slender reptile with its scales and narrow snout, the more he saw a resemblance to the monster that attacked their bivouac last night. Here before him now sat the monster's baby.

But John had more pressing problems than that small reptile. Where were the others? Had they survived? He was now downriver quite a ways and back on the original side from which they commenced. Then there was the palace guard. Were they all killed by the dragon? If there were any survivors, they would probably stagger back to Edgewood, which would mean they were heading his way.

As he pondered these things he could not help but notice the dragon lying with its long snout resting on the ground, its big eyes staring at him. It made him uneasy, and it also made him groggy. Soon all he wanted to do was sleep. John shook off the feeling, stood up, and collected some more dead branches to throw on the fire. Wherever he went, the dragon's piercing eyes followed him relentlessly. John figured it must be afraid of being alone out here.

The boy sat back down and threw the sticks of wood he collected on the fire. Still he was left with the interminable question: what to do next? Overcome with weariness John laid back and fell asleep. He dreamed of a voice which kept repeating, '*Wake up.*' He struggled to do so. At last John opened his eyes in time to see the baby dragon jump into the river with his sword in its mouth.

"Hey!" John cried out, "Where are you going with that!" He could do nothing but look on as the small lizard swam to the middle of the river with its head raised above the surface bearing John's sword in its mouth. Then the small dragon released the sword and it sank.

The boy looked on helplessly. "Why did you do that?" he asked rhetorically. He wondered if the creature thought he was doing John a favor, or whether it didn't know what it was doing, or sensed it was in danger from the sword.

The little dragon began swimming back to shore. Again that voice John heard in his sleep now returned, though still inaudible, '*Run!*'

The dragon was swimming swiftly back to shore. John now realized why the dragon took his sword...in order to kill him! John ran until he found a branchy tree. The dragon did not have claws needed to climb, so the boy quickly ascended as high as he dare go. The little dragon circled the tree a couple of times and then laid itself down and waited.

John knew he had to take some sort of action soon. The longer he waited the more hungry and thirsty he would become and invariably weaker to do anything. A plan began to form in the boy's mind. It was his only hope, and he would just get one chance. If he failed, he would die.

John climbed down so that he was just high enough to be out of the reach of the infant reptile. The small animal watched with interest and was no longer afraid of the boy without a weapon.

John suddenly jumped and landed behind the creature. The dragon turned its head, its teeth bared ready to strike; but John quickly grabbed the long tail and swung the animal around as hard as he could smashing its head against the tree, breaking its frail neck instantly.

He let go of the limp animal and it fell to the ground - dead. The question that had plagued him was forefront again: What should he do now? As if things couldn't get worse he heard footsteps coming from behind. The boy swung around and saw Dresler walking out of the deep woods.

John stepped back startled and at the same time relieved – a familiar face was very welcomed. "It's you," he stuttered in surprise. "What are you doing out here?"

"I have come to give an answer to your question."

"To what question?" John asked, his mind drawing a blank on whatever he had been pondering and then he added, "Franklin believed it was you who put the scroll behind the tavern."

"I did."

"Who are you – a messenger from the White King?" John asked skeptically, assuming a king would not send an old man on such an errand.

"I am the king's son."

John looked quizzically at Dresler. "How old is this king?"

"He has no age. He always has been."

"Your father is one of the gods," John said in amazement and in wonder that a son of a god would deem him worthy to visit.

"He is the supreme God."

"I always thought there had to be one more powerful than all others."

"He is the only God. The other gods are merely lesser powers."

John stood quietly thinking on this and then finally spoke, "Why has your father called us out of Fartherwood to travel through the wilderness?"

"These lesser gods are gathering an army to storm the gates of Vale as you know from the words of the scroll. They will be stopped."

"By whom?"

"By those that I will send, but it will not be easy. The barbarians from the forest of Genadar are led by a supreme evil spirit called the prince of Genadar who rules over the lesser powers. It is under his leadership that the fortress of Vale will be attacked."

"Was this prince responsible for the bears, the wolves, and the dragons?"

"Those animals were mere animals of the wild – even the dragon of the deep wilderness, but the prince cast a spell on them to do his bidding."

John then wondered and asked, "What about a man called Banebreath?"

"He is a soldier of the prince. He is still around – beware." John then noticed a concerned look on Dresler's face as he stared at the dead dragon. "You need to be more careful John."

The boy then bristled somewhat in his own defense, and said, "This dragon had saved my life. How was I to know it meant to kill me?"

"I am not scolding you John. Just beware - their deception is great. It is their strongest weapon. You see the dragon only saved your life in order to remove the sword. It feared the power you now could wield. Once the sword was gone you were no threat or so it thought."

"But if it wanted me dead, then it should have left me drift into the rapids. I surely would have died there!" he exclaimed with utter disbelief at Dresler's erroneous conclusion.

"Maybe not," said Dresler. "Luther lived."

John's face lit up. "Luther is alive?"

"Yes, he has rejoined Franklin and Brandish."

"Then Franklin and Brandish too – both alive! Is the dragon dead?"

"Yes, Franklin killed it. But enough about them – I came to talk about you."

John noticed the serious look on Dresler's face. The boy slowly lowered his head in shame. "I have failed Franklin three times – with the bears, the wolves, and now with the dragon. I have been found wanting and incompetent."

"On the contrary, John, just the opposite…I have found you brave, loyal, and faithful. When everyone deserted Franklin, you still believed. You stayed with him in spite of the immense danger. Your value was being there with him. Your presence and friendship helped sustain Franklin more than you can measure. However your journey northward is over."

"Am I to go back to Fartherwood?" he asked sorrowful at such a dreadful conclusion to his adventure.

"No, you are going to Edgewood. I am sending you to Harbinger and Quayfear."

"But Brandish told us they were prisoners held in Edgewood."

"They are but the emissary is treating them well and will take a liking to Harbinger. You must tell them everything I have told you."

John noticed an inflection of urgency in Dresler's voice, and he asked, "After I find Harbinger and Quayfear – then what?"

"Harbinger will be told where he must go. You must go with him. Do not leave Edgewood without Harbinger and Quayfear… and a sword. You will need one."

John then glanced at the river. "Well," he said, while shrugging his shoulders, trying to lighten his stupid mistake, "there was nothing special about that sword anyway."

"No, there wasn't John. It was just a sword, and the next sword you find will be just another sword. What makes it special is not found in the sword itself nor in you but in the one who empowers it. Go now. You must hurry. Three of the palace guards and Kingsley hid from the dragon's onslaught. They are returning to Edgewood. It is imperative you stay ahead of them."

"Here," Dresler said and tossed him a sack with food in it. John caught the sack and flung it over his shoulders. Dresler turned and started back into the woods.

John just stood there in awe, the son of the great God disguised as some old beggar had spoken to him. Dresler stopped and turned around. John half expected some final words of encouragement, but Dresler looked sternly at the boy and spoke, "Move quickly. Now go!"

*

Nine days after his language lessons started with Marshstench the Baron sat as usual in a broad circle for his evening meal with the chief's family along with his close friends and advisors. During the daylight hours Durkel had spent most of his time with the beautiful Marshstench who he found to be quite a taskmaster plodding through common nouns, verbs, and adverbs; adjectives and idioms until he had a pretty good grasp of the language and could hold down a basic conversation.

The Baron would practice speaking to those who sat by him but tonight as he sat around the circle he was quiet. His thoughts were elsewhere.

Since the Baron's first language lesson with Marshstench, he exercised an interest in a woman for the first time in his life. He had previously never looked beyond his own nose when it came to relationships. Durkel was enough for himself, but now there was a desire to include another. It was a foreign sensation to him but a pleasant one.

The chief of the tribe named Stat called out to get the Baron's attention, "Durkel!"

He turned his head towards the voice. The chief pointed to a new member of the band who had not been present at the dinner before. The Baron eyed the man reverently. He was tall and muscular and sat with an air of authority, but this interloper did not set the Baron at ease, and Durkel's curiosity changed to suspicion. Like, himself, this man appeared to him as an outsider. The burly man visually fit in with the present company, but there was something - he could not say what but something that caused alarm. His aura reminded him of someone he knew…but who?

Suddenly Durkel was brought back to the present moment, hearing Stat speak, "I want you to meet a new tribesman who has proven to be an efficient leader. His name is Stumprot."

Stumprot raised his mug of ale as if to salute his new friend. Durkel did likewise. Just then he remembered the face – this was the man who led him into the keep in Genadar. There he had met someone simply called Number Two in what seemed to be a most unusual consult, especially since his buffoon-like presence did not speak much for the prince.

Stumprot has been sent to me as was Sandgrit…by the Prince. What is he here for but to assure I do not become a rogue warrior? What fools! As if I would make my move this early on. Let him watch and observe a most loyal servant to the prince.

11

Wasted Trip

The grounds behind the walls of Edgewood were muddy from the recent rainfall. There were tufts of yellowish grass which grew haphazardly amongst the constant flow of foot traffic. The emissary walked along with his head bowed thinking of the dream Harbinger had of his encounter with the Baron and his own incident in Pinewood, the quaint hamlet or whatever it was or wasn't.

He glanced up and saw Harbinger on the rampart gazing at the vast stretch of wilderness. Page ascended a stone stairway built against the wall. When he stepped onto the six foot wide passage that followed the perimeter of the large rectangle castle, Harbinger turned his way.

Page initiated. "What do you see that is so interesting – a new species of trees?"

Harbinger chuckled. "No, but the palace guards have been gone five full days. I would have expected by now that Merrill would have sent someone back to fill us in on their progress."

"Do you think something has happened?"

"I don't know, and I also don't know why you and your men did not burst into laughter during my questioning when my only defense for not killing the Baron's knights was what I was told in a dream. The tension in the room was quite evident when I referred to a prince in Genadar."

"That is because we have heard of this prince from the Baron's squire."

"How deep does this intrigue go, my lord. I'm sorry you got dragged into this."

"Let me inform you Harbinger I had no intention of going to the testing grounds this year. I'm nearing the end of my duties as King Fenelon's emissary. It is a job for a younger man. I have been grooming Merrill for the position, but lately I have found him lacking in the qualities needed. Mind you, he is an excellent officer and would remain so, but I have my doubts as to his leadership skills beyond the station he has reached.

"One afternoon, about three months ago in the palace of our king, I lay my head down to rest in one of the informal studies and dreamt that I would find a suitable replacement for the future emissary in Fartherland. When I awoke, I thought long and hard on this...that maybe it was an omen, that I should make the trip to Fartherwood to the testing grounds and that some young man with great potential would be revealed to me, someone who could fill the seat of the emissary. As it happened, I never even made it to the testing grounds. I would think twice the next time of seeing an omen in a dream. It was a wasted trip."

"It seems hardly wasted, my lord."

"Perhaps not, though I'm still at a loss as to my successor. I will appoint Merrill against my better judgment if I can find no other." Page was now silent and gazed onto the open field which led down to the river bank. "I'm also at a loss Harbinger as to my next move. I suppose we just wait."

"Pardon my saying, my lord, but tomorrow you should send some men upriver to see if there is at least any obvious sign of mishap."

Page smiled and replied, "Perhaps I will."

*

Lady Kettery stood on the dock making arrangements with a merchant sailing downriver to Driftwood two days hence. For the last five days she had been trying to secure passage with any merchant going to Fartherwood along the Northern Way, but it was rare that any merchants from this area would have any business so far west. So Lady Kettery finally resigned herself that the only means back was the way they came.

After haggling with the merchant to take them to Baywood after dropping off his goods at Driftwood, Lady Kettery walked away pleased with the price and pleased to get Beth back; but it disturbed her when she noticed Driscoll standing a ways off waiting to speak with her. He approached.

"It seems due to no fault of your own my lady that Ursula is back with us," he began. "Is she going to stay, and more importantly is she going to stay on as head servant?"

"The only thing that you have revealed to me so far Driscoll is that you are desperate, and you make no qualms of letting me know it. Ursula was in a desperate situation, yet she said nothing and did not reveal her dismay and did not become rattled. It does not bode well for you Driscoll."

Lady Kettery then turned and walked away, leaving the forlorn cook standing on the dock alone and angry.

*

Beth sat on the edge of one of the piers soaking in the stillness of the moment, pondering her recent decision. While traveling downriver she had thought of nothing but working for the Duchess of Dogwood; but when she had come in sight of her lady behaving so out of character, waving her hands jubilantly over her head, Beth then felt a tinge of guilt having dwelt on leaving her mistress. She now resigned herself to staying at the manor. For some unexplained reason it seemed like it was where she belonged. Besides, she was never sure of the Duchess' motives.

Ursula sat in her room staring out the second floor window at Beth who sat quietly and seemingly content, dangling her feet in the waters of the River Green. She seemed to have found some secret to life; either that or there was no secret, just an obvious answer only the simple could recognize.

For Ursula life was not so simple. The knight she liked was up in Edgewood but for how long and how much longer would it be until Lady Kettery finds passage back to Fartherwood and puts an end to what little hope she ever had of marrying Baker.

Still, things were not as bad as they might have been. Lady Kettery had not mentioned what had happened in Baywood; and since then, her lady had not spoken degradingly to her. It was rather pleasant and yet strange.

Ursula heard the door swing open. She heard Lady Kettery say, "Please come with me."

Please! The two walked downstairs and out into the open air. Ursula glanced suspiciously at her mistress but nothing was revealed beyond that hard crust of a shell. Ursula did not know what to expect. Her mistress was capable of anything. They traversed down one of the streets without speaking, moving away from the river.

Finally the elder woman spoke: "So what have you learned?"

"That you cannot be trusted, my lady."

"Then why are you still in my company."

"It matters not if I can trust you. What matters is that you can trust me…and you can," she added, making a smooth transition back to the nest if the play on the knight from Dogwood failed to materialize.

"You have answered shrewdly because you are also hoping your knight will return to Wilderwood soon. We leave the day after tomorrow," Lady Kettery snapped, abruptly turned and walked away.

*

The river was dark and quiet at this late hour. The candles and oil lamps in the taverns, guilds, inns, and dwellings along the river had been snuffed out hours ago. A small woman appeared floating on the water. She had long straight black hair. She was floating towards shore, towards a particular boat. When she got to her destination, her body rose from the water and beneath her body was what appeared to be a smooth rock. Suddenly there was a slight splash as a crusty head bopped above the surface. The turtle opened its mouth and bit into the hull of a boat releasing the splintery fragments into the water – then it took another bite and another until it was through the hull. The river started to pour into the bottom of the boat. The girl gently patted the snapper on its head, and the head disappeared beneath the surface as the turtle swam away with the young woman riding atop.

Once downriver it paddled to the embankment, and the girl got off the shell, gave it a couple of taps and off it swam. The girl with the long black hair traversed along a narrow trail that wound along the river and led to the city. As she walked the soaking cold water evaporated instantly, her clothes and hair were dry. Her footsteps made no sound.

12

Mama's Mad

It was the beginning of the second day since John had seen Dresler. He noticed the huge pine jutting out into the rapids from the opposing embankment. After a brief respite munching on a couple of apples from the sack of food Dresler had given him, he commenced downriver.

The female dragon sniffed frantically along the riverbank. The scent of its young was near, as well as John's scent. As she swung her huge head her jaundice-colored eye caught a glimpse of her baby lying alongside the trunk of a tree. It quickly plodded through the undergrowth with its snout to the ground and nudged the lifeless creature. With a quick jerk it raised its enormous head and gave such a loud and mournful cry that its faint echo reached Edgewood.

Daria stood upon a rampart on the North wall gazing at the ground below wondering how Beth was faring with Lady Kettery. She quickly raised her head upon hearing a faint unworldly noise coming from the quiet wood. A guard who stood a short ways from Daria heard it too. "What was that?" he asked Daria. Daria shrugged her shoulders and started down the stairs to find Page and Harbinger.

Daria led them to the spot where she had heard the noise. They stood atop the rampart staring intensely upriver but it was quiet. The woods looked peaceful. Page asked the guard on duty. "Did you hear it?"

"I heard it too, my lord, but the more I think on it, the more I believe it was just thunder."

"Outside of a few high clouds the weather is fair."

"What else could it be?"

Harbinger interjected, "The knights Montague sent out yesterday must have clearly heard that sound. Perhaps they will shed some light into this mystery."

"Yes," said a frustrated emissary, "more waiting."

*

The loud frightful roar had nearly paralyzed the four knights Montague had sent upriver to search for the palace guards. "What in Fartherland was that?" asked Hadrian.

"Some kind of creature!" Brom responded.

The knight in charge spoke. "I think we have our answers as to what happened to the palace guards. No need to go any farther…back to warn the others!"

At the same moment Merrill along with the two remaining palace guards and Kingsley stopped in their tracks when the not-so-distant roar startled their mindless plodding downriver. Ewar gasped, "You were right, Merrill, there is another one!"

"It must be looking for its mate."

"And it may be heading this way!" Ewar declared. "There is no defeating this beast outside of some kind of magical sword… that we don't possess!"

Kingsley interjected, "The roar of the beast came from downriver. If it's going to Edgewood, we will not get there in time to warn them."

"But at least," replied Ewar sardonically, "we will get there in time to help bury the dead."

"The walls of Edgewood are high and thick," corrected Merrill. "Do not be too hasty in your conclusion."

"But are they high and thick enough."

John's heart skipped a beat when he heard the resonating sound. "Another dragon," he gasped. Although John had taken Dresler's command to heart, suddenly the task to meet up with Harbinger and Quayfear became more urgent, more necessary. He now realized this was no longer an adventure or a lark or an excuse to leave Fartherwood. This was life and death. Everything now mattered. Any delay, any mishap led to consequences in which other lives were drastically affected.

*

The next morning Lady Kettery looked out of her second story window upon the River Green and saw some commotion below. The merchant she hired to take them to Baywood was speaking to some knights and appeared very upset. She went to find Driscoll. "Wake up!" Lady Kettery called out.

Driscoll jerked his head up.

"Get down to the docks. The man I hired to take us downriver is very disturbed and speaking to some knights. Find out if there is a problem."

"Yes, my lady," Driscoll said, eager to show his dependability.

Lady Kettery saw that the cook had no trouble getting involved in the conversation. They seemed to be filling him in. He began nodding his head. Driscoll glanced up at her room, then thanked the knights and headed towards the inn.

"What is it?" she asked and without waiting, answered for herself, "He is in trouble with some magistrate?"

"No, my lady, someone had deliberately sunk his boat last night."

"Driscoll, I do not want to grow old and die here. I want to go home!"

"And home you shall go, my lady. Fear not, I will secure us passage."

"Find Blackrose and take her with you. She did a good work in Baywood getting us a very reasonable rate."

"My lady, I am quite capab…"

"Do as I say!"

"Of course, my lady," he stated reverently and dismissed himself from her presence.

*

By late afternoon the trees cast long shadows over the flowing river. The four knights of Edgewood who heard close up the unearthly roar rowed furiously back towards the fortress, even though the stark quiet of the wilderness had resumed.

"Look," said Brom pointing towards the riverbank, "a girl!"

Hadrian speculated, "She must have strayed too far from the hamlet and got lost."

"What is a damsel doing this far upriver from Edgewood?" the knight in charge declared in almost disbelief at this outlandish scene. He was puzzled why she did not wave frantically, or become animated yelling for help. She simply stood up straight, her posture perfect - her clothes clean and tidy as if she had been waiting for them.

Hadrian waved and shouted, "Stay there! We'll come and get you."

Then they saw the dark haired girl point at them.

"Look!"

The others saw it too. Splash after splash resounded along the river's edge as if large boulders were rolled from the embankment into the water. Yet upon a second glance they could see they weren't boulders but large turtles, the hump of their dark shells protruding above the surface and moving swiftly towards them.

Hadrian then noticed the girl pointing downriver and more snappers plopped into the waters swimming out a distance and then floated randomly appearing as large rocks jutting above the surface to hinder the boat from passing. "Grab an oar Oliver! We need to steer through this labyrinth of shells!"

"We cannot avoid them all!"

The boat hit one - bounced and hit another, giving the flank of turtles time to catch up to them. At once all the charging turtles raised their heads above the surface.

"Brom, defend!" the one in charge hollered and withdrew his sword. "You two keep moving us forward." The rowers kept plying their way through a maze of solid obstacles adrift before them.

Hadrian tried pushing one aside when suddenly its head popped up from below, grabbed the oar in its mouth, and with a quick snap of its neck pulled it from the startled knight and swam away. The other knight kept rowing with long hard thrusts. In spite of his comrade's efforts Hadrian noticed they made little progress until he realized the boat was simply adrift. "Raise your oar out of the water!" Hadrian ordered. Oliver lifted it. "No!" declared Hadrian. They both looked at the oar awestruck. The paddle had been bitten off.

Hadrian glanced at Oliver with a look of dread. The riverbank was so close but there was no way of getting there. He then caught the eye of his superior. "Don't just sit there. Help defend. Get up!"

The two rowers now withdrew their swords ready to fight alongside their comrades against the wave of snappers. Hadrian was amazed at the length of the necks of these animals when fully extended. He swung his sword lopping off the head of one before it could bite into his leg.

Then dull thuds resounded in his ears. He lowered his head and saw some of the boards bend inward as a few turtles began ramming the boat, rocking it wildly. The officer in charge lost his balance, reached out and clutched Hadrian for balance, though the swaying of the boat only assured that both would be dragged overboard. The knight clutched the officer's hand and yanked it off of him and then letting go, he saw the frightened face of his commander staring up at him in disbelief as the man fell backwards into the water. And no sooner the blood of the man spurted out in every direction as he cried out in utter torment as a mass of wide open jaws dug chunks of flesh from him. Hadrian could only gape in disbelief at what was happening to them.

Another turtle grabbed the blade of Oliver's sword in its mouth and pulled. "Let it go!" Hadrian hollered but Oliver yanked back hard. The teetering of the boat threw the knight off balance, and he was pulled into the water. The two remaining knights heard the tortured cries as the creatures ruthlessly chomped at their friend. When the screaming ended all they saw were pieces of Oliver floating downstream.

With stark anger and rage Brom swung his sword wildly at these reptiles and caught the neck of one, sending the head flying. Hadrian looked on as the useless brownish shell floated idly away amidst a river dotted with dark brownish shells. There were too many of them.

The smashing of the turtles from underneath was relentless. Hadrian glanced down at the water that now seeped into the boat between the boards when suddenly an atrocious head smashed through near the keel and grabbed his ankle. "Aiee," he cried, "help me!" He reached for Brom, but his fellow knight pulled away.

Brom glanced around at the turtles converging on the sinking boat and heard the cry of his comrade as the man's ankle was slowly being gnawed from off his leg. Brom threw down his sword, jumped out of the boat, and ran atop the protruding shells as far as he could before he dove into the water and swam towards shore.

He's not going to make it! All Hadrian saw were Brom's arms fly up in the air as two turtles caught up to him, each grabbing an ankle. They pulled the knight to the bottom, and there they held him. He could merely stand in the miry muck until the air from his lungs was gone. When they finally let him go his body floated to the surface. The remaining knight saw it pop up as a cork and drift downriver.

Hadrian cried for help as the boat began to sink and the gnarly creatures awkwardly climbed over the stern, feasting on the young knight as he screamed in agony. The last thing he saw was the girl along the shore waving goodbye.

*

Merrill saw before him blackened burnt twigs and brush and scattered fish bones. "Someone has camped here."

"It is most likely a hermit," Kai deduced.

"No," declared Ewar, "the tracks here indicate a man and a boy: John and probably Franklin with the magic sword. The other two perhaps are dead."

"But the Fartherwoods were on the other side of the river," Kai mentioned.

Merrill gazed across the mighty Green and spoke, "Somehow they have crossed over to this side, and are heading downriver, which indicates they have abandoned the quest."

"Look at this!" blurted out Kai upon noticing the baby dragon lying against a tree. "It is a miniature thing of the creature that attacked us. Franklin must have killed it."

Ewar, recalling the dragon's wrenching roar they heard earlier, spoke somberly, "And Mama's mad."

*

John came to the place where the palace guards had abandoned their three boats to continue their pursuit on foot. Dusk was setting in. Behind him he heard intermittent thumps. The creature was near. John hopped in one of the boats and paddled towards the other side of the river, safe from the searing flames. He could see a dark looming outline walking along the bank. Swiftly the dragon turned his head, glaring at him; but John, recalling the mesmerizing gaze of the infant dragon, turned away. The black silhouette of looming death disregarded him for now and continued its elongated strides towards Edgewood where it knew the boy was heading.

13
Walls High and Thick

Montague, the commander of castle Edgewood, strode across the grounds until he found the emissary impatiently pacing alone in the great hall. "My lord," he called. Page looked up but said nothing. "My lord," Montague repeated, "come quickly!"

"What is it?"

"A fisherman found one of my knights washed along the banks of the Green...dead. But killed in a most gruesome manner."

"Show me."

The sun was setting, and the path Montague led the emissary down was narrow and windy. It cut through to a shallow inlet where the boys from the village liked to fish.

"This way...over here," declared Montague as the two stepped through the muck along the periphery of the fen.

"Witness, my lord, the horrendous sight!" Page gazed in disbelief. The body was marred and chewed. "I had sent out four of my best knights, my lord. Do you think your guards suffered the same fate?"

"It is possible."

"What weapon could have done such a thing?"

"None that I know of. This is not the work of our enemies, the Barman's, across the Dark Mountains. This is beyond even their cruelty."

"My lord, we have all heard tales of dragons in the deep wilderness but have never seen one. Could that be what we are dealing with?"

Page did not indulge Montague's speculation, but stated abruptly, "I want archers on the walls all night and through

tomorrow. Then locate Baker, Quayfear, and Harbinger. Send
them to my room – immediately!"

"Yes, my lord, at once."

*

The oil lamp burned brightly upon the emissary's desk. The
furniture along the perimeters of the room cast shadows against
the walls. Harbinger, Baker, and Quayfear rapped upon the
door. Page bid them entrance.

"What is the latest development?" questioned Harbinger
referring to the archers on the walls.

"Are we being attacked?" Quayfear asked.

The emissary answered cautiously, "I don't know. One of
the knights from the castle we sent out two days ago was found
dead along the banks of the river just north of the village. His
body mutilated, which is why I have called you here. That
knight's death was no ordinary one, and since you Harbinger
had related a very strange dream you had had, I want to fill you
in on an even stranger occurrence that Baker, I, and Kai, along
with Ulric experienced in the fief of Dogwood."

The emissary told of the episode with occasional nods and
affirmations from Baker and some wide-eyed, opened-mouth
expressions from Quayfear who also was hearing it for the first
time. He then gave Harbinger and Quayfear a brief dissertation
on the meeting with the Duke of Dogwood. After concluding he
asked, "Well, what say you?"

Harbinger responded: "A collusion of the kings of the
West preparing to march against the Realm sounds logical and
reasonable since the scroll mentions an attack on Vale. However,
the scroll oddly does not mention the kings in the West. The
Baron in my dream made no mention of the kings in the West.
Your bizarre incident in Pinewood involves some spirit being
from Genadar. Four knights of Edgewood are brutally killed on
the River Green, far and away from the western kings; so I think

we can rule out any sound and reasonable conclusion, pointing to the kings in the West."

Quayfear noticed a gleam of satisfaction come over the emissary at Harbinger's response. Page cleared his throat and simply said, "I agree. Now to the purpose of your summons." Page then stood up and ordered Quayfear to sit at his desk.

Quayfear hesitated.

"Go on."

The chunky scribe glanced over at Harbinger and his friend nodded. Quayfear sat and stared at a blank scroll and quill and ink neatly arranged on the desk.

"It doesn't work if you just look at it."

"Yes, my lord, of course." Quayfear took hold of the quill.

"In the event that I am hurt or killed," Page began, "I want this scroll delivered to King Fenelon. It is to say that I, Page, the emissary of the Midland Realm here designate Harbinger of Fartherwood to be the next emissary to his majesty."

The three were silent, though Quayfear kept writing. Harbinger, after a pregnant pause, spoke. "My lord, I don't understand. I am a prisoner. I am not even a knight of the Realm. I have not proved myself a viable candidate. Besides I cannot accept such a position without Merrill here."

"Merrill may be dead, but if he isn't, you are still my first choice. I know you are young and have a lot to learn and experience. In the experience department Merrill is ahead of you, but he has had much time to learn and is unable to assume the position of full leadership. He has excelled as far as he can and is quite capable where he is."

"Quayfear," the emissary said gravely peering down at him from where he stood, "you are no longer a scribe under Baron Durkel. You now are Harbinger's scribe and Baker you are no longer a knight of Dogwood, but a palace guard." Page noticed that all three were overwhelmed at their promotions. "Well," he continued with a sly grin, "if you don't want them, let me know now, so I can make other arrangements."

Harbinger spoke for the three of them. "My lord, we are honored to receive such positions and status with our King, but we all pray that nothing befalls you my lord."

"Even if nothing happens to me, nothing changes. When we return to The Great City, I personally will assign you these titles before our king. It is time for me to resign."

Suddenly Quayfear noticed a stern gaze from the emissary, drawing his attention. "You will hold onto that scroll. Do not let it out of your possession. No one else but you three are to know about it." The emissary looked hard at Harbinger. "And that includes Daria."

"Of course, my lord."

"Very good," the emissary concluded and pulled something small from his pocket. "Melt some wax Baker and I will seal it. This will verify that it is from me."

"Enough said - now get some sleep, and let us pray that if this attack of whatever it is comes, it does not do so at night."

*

Baker sat by himself in the crowded common room and ate a hearty dinner of boar and potato stew with chunks of aged cheese and stale bread washed down by a mug of dark ale while contemplating his new position. After which, he got up and stepped outside the warm room heated by two large brick ovens on either end. The air was brisk. Even from behind the high walls he could see a beautiful sunset was in the offing, so he headed up the stairway to get a glimpse from the ramparts. There was another knight on guard duty in the far corner of the wall near the West Tower.

Baker ignored him and leaned against the parapet gazing at the vast quiet forest. The low angle of the sun illuminated the ceiling of trees lost in a distant horizon. He didn't notice the guard who had been standing at the far corner of the wall suddenly standing next to him.

"Oh!" Baker exclaimed, "I didn't hear you approaching."

"It matters not that you did not hear me coming. What matters is you hear me now."

"I don't know you."

"My name is Fairhaven, and I serve the White King whom you have heard of from the scroll found in Fartherwood."

Baker eyed him with suspicion as to how he was able to converge on him so quickly from the West Tower to where he now stood. He was suspicious of any kind of abnormal behavior since his time in the quaint hamlet. "Why should I believe you?"

"I know of what you experienced in Pinewood and that you have heard of the Prince of Gender from the Duke of Dogwood."

Baker, in amazement, burst out, "It is Page you want to see! Let us find him."

"That is not necessary. You have served faithfully under the authority of the emissary, but you are to leave immediately for Driftwood and warn the Earl there of an imminent attack upon his city from a fire-breathing dragon."

"Does such an animal exist? Are they not stories told to frighten children into obedience?"

Fairhaven ignored the comment. "A boat awaits you with two rowers. There are enough supplies to take you straight through to the city. These men will require no sleep nor will they grow weary at their task."

Baker, now realizing the existence of dragons was not deemed worthy of discussion, said, "Pardon me for saying, my lord, but it would seem unlikely that the earl will take my warning to heart."

"You are now a palace guard of the Midland Realm. Therefore he will deem you audience." Fairhaven did not stay to give further elaboration but abruptly turned and hurried down the stairs, leaving the knight from Dogwood to contemplate this latest turn of events.

In order to put things into perspective Baker hurriedly reviewed in his mind his brief history. He had gone from a mere knight of Dogwood to assisting the king's emissary and recently to a position in the palace guard and now brought into service under some god unfamiliar in Fartherland called the White King.

He could not deny that his life had unexpectedly been catapulted into positions of responsibilities which he deigned he was unprepared for, but this latest assignment from this dubious soldier called Fairhaven was too much to accept at face value. This was information that must be passed on to his superior.

Baker hurried down the stairs and set his sights on the common room in the keep where Page was still dining when he heard a clear deep voice speak his name. The young knight turned and in the gray twilight behind the walls he saw the silhouette of a man hunched over. He appeared to be a common beggar, elderly.

"Who are you?" Baker called out nervously, "And how do you know my name?"

The elderly man did not move but waited for Baker to approach him. "My name is Dresler, the son of the White King. I have known you for a long time."

Baker wondered how that could be. "Did you know my mother and father?"

"Yes."

Baker found this answer rather preposterous, but with all that he had experienced since leaving Fartherwood, he did not pursue it. "What do you want?"

"To instruct you that the gate is that way," Dresler said while lifting his arm and extending a finger.

Baker blinked, and spoke in bewilderment, "Then you know of my meeting with Fairhaven."

Dresler did not respond, but said, "You were instructed to leave immediately and that means without contacting anyone, not even a goodbye. Your concern for Page and Edgewood is justified but you must understand that the fate of Edgewood is not in your hands, nor has it been left to the outcome of random events. You are responsible for what has been entrusted to you."

"Then will you inform Page of the change in plans."

"There has been no change in plans," Dresler stated firmly, turned and walked away into the darkness which now enveloped the grounds behind the walls. The sun had set.

Baker shuttered, not only from a quick drop in temperature, but of his sudden mission, without overseer, without clarity... why him? His legs were shaky, and he stumbled with the first few steps, but slowly he regained a normal stride.

The guards were readying to close the gate. "Sir," one of the guards said, addressing Baker, "we are closing the gate and you won't be able to reenter until daybreak."

"Understood," was all Baker said and headed down the road towards the village until he heard the sound of chains clanging and iron wheels turning as the heavy gate was lowered. He hesitated, stopped, and turned. The gate appeared as a large mouth yawning shut, preparing for a good night's rest, keeping those behind its walls safe from those things that creep and lurk in the shadows of the forest. Baker then turned from the closed fortress and restarted towards the river where he was told a boat awaited him with two rowers.

*

After an hour of gazing at the dark quiet shore, Baker lay down in the skiff looking up at the black dome above spattered with far away stars, but as distant as they were he saw order, pattern, serenity, unlike what he was going through now. From his uncomfortable horizontal position he listened to the oars gently part the waters, perfectly timed to get the most speed and distance with the least amount of effort. The harmony of the gentle splashes became like a soft lullaby. He wondered if somehow this order, pattern, and serenity could be had down here. Baker closed his eyes and slept.

He awoke to the same perfectly timed oar strokes. The two men showed no fatigue. The darkness was beginning to fade. Baker figured he would try some conversation to learn more about this White King and his servants. "Where do you hale from?" he asked the taller one. The man was thin and frail looking and did not seem built for hours of rowing without end. But he was not troubled by it.

"Mount Forever," he said but offered no elaboration.

"It must be cold. Surely you are pleased to be where the spring weather brings some relief from the icy chill."

"Wherever we are sent, it is good to be there."

Baker assumed by the rower's cheerful disposition, they were unaware of an attack coming upon Driftwood by a fire breathing dragon.

The shorter hefty one who seemed built for the task of rowing and sported an attractive full beard, asked, "Are you not glad to be here?"

"I have not been given much information as to why I am here, so how can I be glad."

"The amount of information is irrelevant when the command comes from the White King."

"Why so?"

The short man cocked his head, looked at Baker in a peculiar sort of way as if what he had said was common knowledge, and spoke, "If you had received all of the information at once, it would only lead to more questions, and those answers would lead to even more questions."

"And besides all that," the tall one interrupted, and spoke, "If all was made known to you from the start, you would be so overwhelmed at what the White King has planned for you, you would not go."

Baker sat up stiffly on his bench and spoke indignantly, "It is for lack of information that I am tempted to abort this mission and return to Edgewood."

"It is not a lack of knowledge that tempts you to quit but fear of moving forward to do what you perceive is impossible."

The short one then stated forthrightly, "Baker, you do not realize what you are capable of. This journey will lead you to that knowledge."

"Having two servants of the White King to assist me will be a source of strength and confidence, so since we are going to be working together, I should know your names."

"I am Placid," said the tall lean one.

"I am Still, but we will not be going with you. We are merely dropping you off at Driftwood."

"Then I am to do this alone…without help!"

"Do not fret," Still encouraged, "the White King does not expect you to do this alone. After the dragon's attack upon the city, you must seek out a man named Driscoll."

"Is he a servant of the White King as yourselves?"

"No,"

"A fellow palace guard?" Baker asked hopefully.

"No."

"A knight stationed in Driftwood then?"

"No, he is a middle-aged overweight ornery self-centered cook."

"Is this the White King's idea of a jest? Of what use will this man be? He sounds more like a burden."

Baker's remark went unanswered and Still merely stated, "You will find him working at a tavern called The High House." Then nothing but silence from the two men.

The two servants of the White King continued to row nonstop, lifting their oars, piercing the surface of the current like an arrow while forcing the oars back with thrusts without exertion moving them closer, every minute, towards the white walls of Driftwood.

*

It was early dawn and a pale grayness greeted the eyes of the men on the ramparts. The dragon was couched down in the woods just beyond the grassy hill below the fortress, its long neck lay on the ground with its head tilted up glaring at the tiny men who somehow managed to slay its mate and kill its baby. The hard plated monster was surprised to see the bowmen awaiting its arrival. The dragon determined it too risky to fly. Its wings were a thin taught web, easily penetrated with arrows. The only way the beast would attack through the air is with the element of surprise and that had been eliminated.

A knight leaned on his elbow looking out over the tall dark grass which swayed silently in a cool pre-dawn breeze. He thought he saw some movement. "Look," he said to the man next to him, "over there."

"I don't see anything."

"It's nothing I guess."

"You're on edge. We all are. The palace guards had left many days ago, and where are they? Four of our own knights sailed upriver soon after, and they have not returned - yet we have been told nothing, and now suddenly the ramparts are full of archers."

"Maybe, because they don't know themselves...look... again – the movement!"

"I don't see..."

"Dragon!" the other knight cried out as a black form tore out onto the open field charging up the hill, its lissome neck snaking through the air as arrows let fly from the walls - then a blast of heat. The two knights felt the sudden rush of heat just before the flames engulfed them and turned them into human brands. The hail of arrows simply bounced off the hard plates. Other knights were ignited along the parapet. Many of the remaining men turned and ran down the stairs clogging it so that the men began tripping over one another, tumbling to the ground.

Montague shouted from below for the knights to stand their ground, but there was total chaos as the long neck hovered above the wall as tongues of fire shot down into the keep, searing some and completely burning others.

Montague tried to maintain order when suddenly a deadened thud resounded over the confusion and frenzy. He quickly turned and faced the wall as he saw the seams between the tightly laid blocks shake and small crumbling fragments of stone dribble to the ground. The dragon was pounding the thick wall with its tail. The smashing of the iron like appendage was relentless. Large sections of stones began to bulge, balancing precariously upon one another until finally the pounding and jolting completely shoved the massive stones out of place. Large sections of wall crashed down on the men below, further adding to the deaths and mayhem inside the keep.

Harbinger and Daria noticed the emissary aiding the wounded. They both shouted but to no avail. Page could not hear. He could not respond. A block of stone fell from above and grazed the emissary's head. He stumbled for a moment before falling over. Harbinger and Daria hurried toward the royal liege. Perhaps he was just stunned. Harbinger fell on his knees and upon turning the emissary's head he saw it was more than a graze, but the emissary was alive. Page opened his eyes. He could barely speak.

"We'll get you out of here," Harbinger said.

"No, if you help me, it will only insure your deaths," he said in a muffled voice. Harbinger had to bend low to hear him. "I have given you your orders. I expect them carried out… understood."

"Yes, my lord."

"Page gave him a weak smile, and said, "It looks like I was wrong. This trip was not for naught." The smile then vanished and his head tilted to the side revealing the bloody smashed skull."

"What did he say?" asked Daria.

Harbinger looked at her and then away, and spoke a lie having sworn not to reveal the actual command and instead said, "Go to The Great City and inform the King of all that has happened."

Just then Daria looked up and another large section of wall tumbled into a heap. A film of dust and dirt rose from the debris giving Harbinger and Daria some cover. They scurried away jumping over charred bodies and tons of strewn rock. When the dust cleared, they saw the beast come through the breach in the wall, its sinewy neck swooping down and catching running men in its cavernous mouth.

"What now?" Daria shouted above the screams and furor.

"Find Quayfear - and then to the river!"

"Should we bother? He might already be dead."

"He must come with us."

"Why?" Daria questioned, puzzled by Harbinger's concern about the scribe in such a dire predicament. "Look," exclaimed Daria, "over there! Is that him?"

Harbinger saw the scribe feeling his way along the outside wall of the armory. He wondered how this was perceived by Quayfear. Were the flames no more than blurry yellow reddish streaks smeared as if on a hastily painted canvas?

Harbinger and Daria forged their way to the scribe. Harbinger spoke, startling the frightened man, "It's me, Quayfear. The emissary is dead!"

"Where is Baker?"

"I don't know. We can't take the time to find him. We must leave now."

"Is there no stopping that thing?"

"It is not our place to find out. We have our orders from the emissary."

Daria took Quayfear's hand but then quickly withdrew it as she heard Quayfear wrenching and throwing up. The atmosphere was ripe with burnt flesh.

"What are we taking him for?" she asked.

Harbinger said nothing but grabbed the scribes hand and led the way. They finally made their way out the gate and hurried down the road towards the river. The hamlet was nearly empty and all the boats gone.

"Now what do we do?" asked Daria. "We are hemmed in against the River Green."

Harbinger glanced upriver and saw a boat round a bend in the river. "What good fortune! One of the knights Montague had sent out has survived."

"He's awfully young," said Daria.

"You're right...I don't believe it. It is John, the boy at the tavern! But where is Franklin?"

The mother dragon stood in the midst of the keep upon its hind legs, its neck stretched high in its glory tolling vengeance for the death of her mate and infant when she noticed that boy again in the boat. The creature let out a roar and ran towards the gate breaking thick wooden boards which splintered into a thousand pieces and the stones above the lentil bounced off the shingled torso as the animal swiftly left the dust and debris behind and trounced towards the river.

Harbinger got into the boat and aided Quayfear and Daria and pushed off. The dock vibrated from the thunder of slamming feet against earth as the dragon hurried towards the river.

14
Flight to Driftwood

The long black form had crushed homes and shops in the village nestled below the castle leaving behind nothing but shattered memories in its wake; and it now wearily trudged along the edge of the river with a desire to enflame Harbinger, Daria, Quayfear, and John but they were beyond its range. It was clear to them that the beast was tiring. It had been awake for two full days and was now spent. Its legs suddenly gave out from under it, and the fire breathing beast collapsed onto the ground exhausted. The ground shook and the waters rippled across the river rocking the boat in a series of undulating waves.

The dragon's breathing was heavy, and it appeared to lay there helpless. But the battle wasn't over. It stared intently at those in the boat and caught Daria's attention. She saw that the dragon's gaze upon her was more than vile hatred. It contained an element of intrigue and power, a power beyond its physical brute strength. Daria glared back at it with great intent as if entering a dual. What she saw frightened and amazed her. The dragon had some mysterious ability to control and manipulate that which she craved for herself.

"Do not look into the dragon's eyes!" John shouted when he saw her staring at its massive form.

She heard him but did not respond. Daria saw something she liked. Whether it was a vision or if it was reality, she could not say, but she saw an irreverent looking man, dressed in puffy colorful garb. He appeared quite preposterous yet apparently possessed great authority. She found herself in a marbled hall, and this buffoonery of a jolly carefree fellow sat upon a throne. She noticed though that his face warranted respect in spite of his outward facade.

He asked her to come forward. She hesitated and then found herself glancing at Harbinger who stood by her side. She felt torn, but her mind was firm. She wanted more. Daria slowly walked towards this king. When she stood before the dais, the young maiden turned around and saw that Harbinger looked very tiny, no bigger than a mouse. The man on the throne extended his arm but stopped short of touching her. Daria reached out and grabbed his hand, and she was yanked in.

"Daria!" Harbinger shouted. When he saw her face aglow, mesmerized and absorbed, he shook her. He knew what was happening to her. He had been there in his dream with the Baron. Her body was with them but her mind was not.

When she awoke from her trance Daria was staring into Harbinger's face. She stated succinctly as if nothing out of the ordinary had happened, "I am fine! Now get us out of here."

Harbinger realized she had seen something. She had been faced with a temptation as he had. There was no point in confronting her now. She would need time to contemplate what had just happened.

"The beast needs to rest," Harbinger said, glaring at the black leathery heap upon the bank of the river. "That allows us some time."

"Yes," said Quayfear, "but how much."

The fatigued beast looked on at the small people in the little boat and was unconcerned. Tomorrow morning she would fly downriver and quickly catch up to them and would finish them off in a burst of flame.

"Wait, wait!" cried John, "I can't leave without a sword. The Dresler told me to find you and Quayfear in Edgewood, and I was not to leave without a sword."

"You saw Dresler out here?" questioned Harbinger.

"Yes, I will explain later."

Harbinger suddenly realized that his sword was not with him. "We are without a weapon."

"Look," said Daria, "a body."

Harbinger and John rowed towards the floating corpse. It was a knight of Edgewood, though he was not killed in today's battle. It was not burnt but mutilated. Quayfear turned away unable to look at the grotesque visage. Harbinger reached out and dragged it towards the boat, unclasped the scabbard and sword, and pushed the body away. "Here, it seems a sword has been provided," and handed it to John.

"What are you doing?" questioned Daria in disbelief as she saw him hand over the only means of defense to a fourteen year old boy.

"I know that what I am doing appears reckless and foolhardy but try to understand the scroll that we found, that we designated at first as nonsense, we now believe speaks of a war among the gods. A king's son disguised as a vagrant in Fartherwood is now out here in the wilderness and meets up with John and tells him to find me and Quayfear. Is it a coincidence that John arrived in a boat while the three of us were pressed against the river trapped by the oncoming dragon. So if Dresler wants John to have a sword, there is a reason for it. We must trust the truth even if sound reasoning for it is tossed to the wind."

Daria was speechless and could only look on stunned.

Harbinger went on taking advantage of the shocked pause before the sudden burst of anger which would surely follow. "Daria, the emissary pursued us not because he believed we murdered the knights of Dogwood, but because he believed there was something to this scroll. Since I have begun this journey from Fartherwood things have happened, too many to be called coincidence or serendipitous occurrences."

"What has happened to you?" Daria exclaimed perturbed and disappointed in what she had just heard. "You are not the same man I knew! Far be it from me to have anything to do with this nonsensical scroll you speak of."

Quayfear addressed Daria with aplomb and showed her more respect than she deserved and said, "My lady, we also ridiculed Franklin of such naiveté at the start, but we have seen and experienced too much now to simply disregard it as happenstance - be patient and you too will soon see that this White King and his son are slowly making themselves known to us in their own way, in their own time."

Daria broke out in a fury. "What kind of way is this? A dragon is unleashed upon Edgewood. Good men are burned alive, and this is the method he chooses to reveal his ways as you call them! You may follow his ways, but I will choose another!"

Harbinger realized that Daria was under some kind of spell from this beast. In time she would return to her senses. He then turned to John. "Now tell us about this meeting with Dresler out here in the wilderness."

John began from his and Franklin's parting from the bivouac in which the knights of Dogwood were killed and ending with his subsequent meeting with Dresler. He emphasized that the White King was the God of gods and that he was at war with these lesser powers.

Harbinger and Quayfear were enthralled and excited about their new awareness of this White King. They both wondered how easy it had been to doubt and now how impossible it was to do so.

Daria, however, sat in the boat unmoved and deliberately turned her gaze away from them and towards the dragon who lay along the embankment. Harbinger followed her gaze towards the cruel beast that had laid waste all in its path, and beyond it was the castle looking like a defeated warrior crippled and left aghast and speechless by the power of an unsuspected foe. When their small boat rounded a bend, Harbinger turned his face downriver.

Banebreath looked on in dismay from the shore, and thought, *Forsooth, the knight from Fartherwood and the plump cherubic looking scribe also have received a special sword along with John through their puerile belief in this White King who was foolish enough to send his son here defenseless as a wandering pauper, but Daria is steadfast against it. Those three men do not fully comprehend the power they have access to nor will they be given a chance to find out. It is a shame the obstinate girl will burn with the rest tomorrow, but she must be sacrificed in order to destroy the other three who have obtained a special sword.*

As Harbinger and Quayfear paddled downriver, John stated, "One more thing, the Dresler told me that you, Harbinger, would know our destination."

"I do. It is the Great City. I must see King Fenelon with an important message per order of the emissary." Harbinger realized he spoke too hastily.

"Concerning what," asked Daria, "you did not mention an important message before when I asked you what Page had said."

Harbinger glanced over at Quayfear and back to Daria. "It was told to me in confidence."

"He's dead now. You can tell us."

"I must honor his wishes."

"He is dead. I am alive. Now you must honor my wishes."

"You must trust me Daria," Harbinger stated in a loving tone. "You will soon learn what it is Page spoke of."

"I will not soon learn. I will learn now! You said it was necessary that Quayfear come along...why?" She glared at the scribe. "Tell me what the emissary said!"

"Harbinger and I are bound by an oath."

Harbinger noticed her ire growing. She turned towards him. "You think you're so big with your privileged information, but you're not." She then chuckled knowingly, and said, "But you are actually quite small."

*

The city of Wilderwood was in a state of panic. Those who had escaped the village of Edgewood informed the folks of Wilderwood of the attack. Some grabbed what they could and put them into wagons, heading across the Northern Way. Others pushed and shoved through throngs of people in the streets heading towards the river, crowding into boats weighed down to nearly sinking. Some took refuge in the woods hoping they could remain hidden until the danger passed.

Ursula heard a loud knock on their door and opened it. There stood the fairest young man she ever had seen. Her heart skipped a beat. "My lord, what is happening?" she asked. "Can you tell us?"

Lady Kettery approached the threshold where the man stood quietly in the hallway and spoke hastily and to the point, not particularly caring who he was. "Do you have a boat?"

"Yes, my lady, it is why I am here. You must leave now. Get the other one and follow me."

"Blackrose!" she called. The young servant came out of a room rather hesitantly.

"I was referring to a man, my lady."

"Oh yes, Driscoll, the one who said he would quickly find me passage back to Fartherwood but failed to do so."

"There is more to Driscoll than meets the eye my lady."

"Whatever more there is of Driscoll is of no help. What is going on out there?"

"A dragon has attacked Edgewood and is heading this way."

Driscoll came trotting down the hall having just awoken to the fuss. "What is happening out there?" he asked with the sleep still in his eyes. "And who are you?" he questioned, gazing with distrust at the handsome man.

"My name is Fairhaven, and I have been sent by the king to rescue your party."

"King Fenelon!" Ursula declared flabbergasted.

"No, the White King."

Driscoll's jaw dropped. "The White King from the scroll? That thing is real?"

"Of course it is real."

Suddenly Beth showed up at the door huffing from a sprint up the stairs. She paid no attention to the stranger but declared to Lady Kettery, "My lady there is mayhem below. Rumor is that something dreadful has happened upriver...some kind of an attack upon Edgewood. There is a mass exodus. We must leave the city now."

"And leave you shall," said Fairhaven. "Follow me!" he concluded, turned and headed toward the stairway.

Lady Kettery hesitated and did not move, though not so much out of distrust but of having to follow instead of lead.

"We cannot delay my lady," Ursula said. "This may be our only chance."

"Very well, we shall proceed with caution."

Blackrose piped in. "You speak wisely and with prudence and discernment my lady. We know little about him."

We know little about you, Ursula thought.

Lady Kettery led them down the staircase to meet Fairhaven on the street.

"This way," he stated.

Fairhaven calmly led them through the bedlam down First Street along the docks. Ursula strode alongside her lady. She turned her head and saw Beth with Driscoll who seemed to her disgruntled over his future with Lady Kettery. Blackrose hung back behind them and walked alone, though Ursula found it strange that she wore an odd expression of glee while glancing around at crying children and frightened parents scrambling for escape.

Ahead Ursula observed an outlandish sight. Amongst the hysteria stood an empty boat, though all around were others filled to maximum capacity with people and goods, yet this one remained empty. No one went near it. Fairhaven got in turned and helped Lady Kettery aboard. Ursula waited patiently as the handsome fellow lent her his hand and gently guided her into the boat. He reached out with both hands to aid the cumbersome cook, and then extended a tender hand to Beth. He then turned and said, "We're in."

"Wait," Lady Kettery said addressing Fairhaven. She then raised her voice and shouted to Blackrose, "Hurry! Come along!"

Ursula noticed how Fairhaven did not make a move to help Blackrose into the boat. In fact he seemed not to acknowledge her. Blackrose jumped from the pier into the boat and quietly sat on the bench, saying nothing to anyone, which was not out of character for her at all.

"Now Fairhaven," Lady Kettery stated in her usual exacting tone, "we may leave."

"Where are you taking us," asked Beth?

"Driftwood."

"No, you are not!" Lady Kettery demanded firmly. "You will take us to Baywood. From there we will make our way to Fartherwood. You will be accommodated for your troubles."

"I take orders from the White King and his son, my lady – not you."

"I have never heard of this White King."

Fairhaven gave her a gentle smile. "You will."

Fairhaven paddled the sleek boat down the River Green passing the weightier over crowded boats and soon pulled far ahead of the others. The sun was warm and high. Ursula observed that Lady Kettery tried to remain angry and upset at Fairhaven, but for some reason she was unable to hold her usual disposition.

The former head servant also noticed a substantial difference in her mistress since Beth's return from Edgewood. Lady Kettery seemed more subdued and relaxed, though she would no doubt take her lady's kindness in stride; for she knew from experience things could quickly change, but surprisingly her employment with her lady seemed more secure than ever while Driscoll's efforts to impress Lady Kettery seemed to falter at every turn.

Ursula glanced at Blackrose who remained a bizarre enigma. The young servant had spent every day and every night with them over the last few weeks and still no one knew anything about her except her unquestioning obedience to her lady. She never socialized and was sometimes hard to find, disappearing sometimes for hours. And although Blackrose showed no recalcitrant behavior towards her lady, she averted contact with Fairhaven, a handsome kind man who had saved them from certain death.

Yet Fairhaven's cold reaction to the young servant was just as mysterious when he was so accommodating to the rest of them. There seemed to be something about Blackrose that had gone from the strange and odd to the nefarious and insidious, though there was nothing obvious or direct to connect her to such malevolent conduct.

Ursula noticed two oars clasped to the side of the boat. "Would you like me and Beth to help row," Ursula asked the young man. "I don't mind."

"There may come a time when I will call on you both to help."

"Very well, my lord, just say the word." Though Ursula found Fairhaven attractive, she did not desire him in a romantic sense. He was average height and build. His auburn hair cascaded in gentle waves to rest upon his shoulders. He sported a fair mustache, though not thick and dense as those appearing like a matted hedge on the face of an otherwise attractive man.

Ursula was suddenly taken aback from her pondering as Blackrose abruptly and without a word to anyone stood up in the boat. Ursula was perplexed as she witnessed the dark haired girl standing perfectly erect, poised without a flicker of movement though the boat rocked and swayed with each thrust of Fairhaven's oar. Ursula followed the eyes of this aberrant character as they looked intently towards the river's embankment. Ursula saw nothing.

"What are you doing?" Lady Kettery asked, exasperated at the odd girl's action.

Blackrose for once did not respond to her mistress but kept gazing along the edge of the river. Then without warning she sat down.

"What did you see?" Lady Kettery asked.

"I have been on alert, my lady, since I heard about the attack on Edgewood. I see no reason to become complacent simply because we are with this man, though we are all grateful for his intercession. However, the movement I saw was merely a few beavers about their daily business - no cause for alarm."

Fairhaven gestured towards Ursula and Beth. "It is time to grab an oar. Driscoll, please sit by Lady Kettery."

"I am fine Driscoll," Lady Kettery calmly responded. "Stay where you are."

"Do as I say Driscoll. Your lady will accommodate."

"Lady Kettery, who normally would have resisted a command just for the sake of resistance, surprisingly had no desire to argue with this man, and so she simply acquiesced and said, "Very well, Driscoll."

"Look!" cried Beth. She pointed at a host of beavers chomping away at a few large pine trees at a much accelerated rate. Within moments these giant firs toppled into the river and were carried by the current downstream. Some of the beavers waddled into the river and followed the felled trees. Beth looked at Fairhaven, and questioned, "What is happening?"

"The beavers will direct the logs towards the boat in order to pulverize it into many fragments. Ursula, Beth, I want you to start rowing while I divert the oncoming trees."

The large semi-aqueduct rodents swam swiftly and working together they guided the floating trees towards the small boat. Fairhaven stood at the stern in order to ease the oncoming trees away from them with his oar. Although these massive heavy timbers would not flinch from their designated target under normal conditions, with this man little effort was needed and with just a touch of Fairhaven's paddle and a slight push the giant trees shifted course and harmlessly floated down river. But the number of fallen trees was quickly increasing as more and more beavers joined the ranks.

Lady Kettery looked at her two servants rowing furiously, but Blackrose sat quietly saying nothing; nor had Fairhaven spoken to her once through this whole ordeal. Then without warning or announcement Blackrose stood up and from a fixed standing position jumped out of the boat across ten feet of rolling river to land on one of the trees floating by. Lady Kettery could not believe her eyes as her petite servant girl stood composed and collected, her arms stretched out pointing to several particular trees coming downriver.

"Faster!" Fairhaven shouted to his rowers. He pushed off an oncoming tree headed straight for stern and then turned to push off another one to starboard but was unable to keep it clear and it glided against the side of the vessel throwing Lady Kettery off her bench. Driscoll grabbed her by the waist and caught her before spilling into the river.

Beth's paddle went flying from her grip as the jolt threw her forward and hitting her head against the gunwale she fell unconscious into the water. "Beth!" Lady Kettery screamed and punched Driscoll in the face and flung herself onto the side of the boat and reached as far as she could towards her servant girl. The beavers guided the tree Blackrose stood upon towards Beth, and Blackrose fished the seamstress out of the water and gently placed her on the massive trunk.

Driscoll rallied himself, reached over and pulled Lady Kettery back into the boat as the woman shrieked and cursed Blackrose while vainly grasping at the air as if that would save her helpless seamstress.

Blackrose noticed the beavers had swum their limit and with a gesture of her hand the chase ended, and the trees were left to float wherever the current would carry them. Fairhaven ordered Ursula to stop rowing. He alone would resume guiding the wooden craft.

"Follow them," Lady Kettery declared to Fairhaven when she saw him make no effort to pursue Blackrose.

"I have my orders from the White King not to engage in a dispute. I must deliver you to Driftwood."

"I am not asking you to engage in a dispute! We need to rescue Beth! Where is that fiend taking her?"

"It is impossible to say for certain, but there is good reason to believe that she will be taken to Castle Calamitous."

"It sounds dreadful. And who dwells there?"

"The harlequins of Glendyland, my lady.

"I must insist your plans change. We are four against one. Surely your king will understand."

"This vessel is going to Driftwood."

"Then you will drop the three of us off at the town of Seven. We will attend to Beth ourselves if you will not oblige your services."

"I cannot force you to go to Driftwood, but I beg you to reconsider. My king knows what is best."

"Listen to him my lady," Driscoll urged. "We are all fond of Beth, and of course you most of all, but she is a seamstress. As difficult as this is for me to say, my lady, a seamstress can be replaced."

Lady Kettery glanced at Ursula and Driscoll and then Fairhaven who seemed for whatever reason to be the essence of truth and light and kindness. For reasons she could not determine Lady Kettery without reserve revealed a long kept truth and without regret spoke in great relief, "It is as you say, Driscoll, a seamstress can be replaced - even a gifted one but a daughter cannot."

Lady Kettery glanced quickly at Ursula's expression who seemed more relieved than shocked. Perhaps it was because her iron lady was not so unique and seeing her mistress for the first time as a real woman with an infamous past now gave Ursula an edge that she hadn't counted on.

Lady Kettery noticed that Driscoll was not so startled but rather disappointed at the weakness in his lady – that she could not keep hidden something that revealed her as common and even desperate. He snickered degradingly at the exposed secret and separating himself from her and this futile rescue attempt stated, "I will not go to this castle, nor will I be a part of this 'family' as you call it my lady. I will be obedient to the White King's command and go to Driftwood."

Although Driscoll spoke forthrightly with loyalty for this king, Fairhaven knew Driscoll possessed no such commitment to anyone or anything but himself. Driscoll was a coward and knew Driftwood would be the safest place.

Ursula realized that this latest confession revealed that her lady could be contrite and humble but how long would it last. Her mistress could not be trusted, and now a great opportunity lay before her to be rid of this old lady for good. With her experience she surely could find work as a head servant in Driftwood; yet even so, ultimately these mistresses were all the same, self-serving and demanding. And now with Driscoll abandoning Lady Kettery her position with her lady would be more secure.

"I will attend to you, my lady, as usual. We shall seek out your daughter together." Ursula thought for sure that Fairhaven would change his mind once seeing the boldness of the two women willing to confront alone the evil which awaited them at Castle Calamitous, but Fairhaven was steadfast and said nothing.

Fairhaven looked on curiously as Lady Kettery abruptly removed herself from Driscoll's side and sat down next to Ursula. He expected from her some kind of outrageous command or comment to show everyone she is still in control, still in charge; but Lady Kettery was silent, sitting up straight and proud. Fairhaven realized that it was Lady Kettery's way of boasting that she had someone she could count on when in dire straits. He knew it had been years since she could make such a claim. Fairhaven was touched and pleased.

Driscoll rolled his eyes at the gesture.

*

By end of day Harbinger and his beleaguered company passed Wilderwood. He noticed that many had cleared out of the river city but there were those few obstinate folks who would remain. Harbinger knew that by dawn the dragon would be well rested. The miles they put in front of the beast would count as a mere handbreadth when the great dragon takes to the sky and follows the river south. Harbinger gave the command to keep rowing, taking turns through the night. They made for shore at the break of dawn just beyond the outskirts of Riverwood and would remain hidden in the overgrowth until the dragon passed by.

15

Preparation

That morning Baker entered the gates of Driftwood with the same expression of all first-time visitors because it looked so out of place. It appeared to have fallen from the sky. He goosenecked this way and that, up and down. He was used to Dogwood which had only a small section where the well-to-do flourished, but they remained primarily confined in that area. Here they sprawled down every street. It took a while before Baker remembered why he was here. He enquired where the earl resided.

Placid and Still had provided him with a new outfit suited for a palace guard, though where it came from Baker did not know. He had woken up from a nap and Still handed it to him…a perfect fit. The silver and blue colors were familiar with all the royalty throughout the Realm. He felt more confident.

Baker stood outside the address which was given him. He noticed that as splendid as it was with its columns and elaborate friezes which banded the top of the building like an ornate ribbon, it did not stand out among its neighbors. A large shiny metal knocker with a sculpted face of an animal was fastened to the center of the door. An animal he had only heard of but had never seen called a lion. He had heard that it was referred to as king of the forest where it roamed many miles away in the Southlands. Baker slammed the heavy knocker three times. A servant attended, a male slave, and asked who he was.

"I am Baker, a palace guard, with an urgent message for the earl."

The slave who knew of the palace guard but had never seen one in the city did not hesitate, but went immediately to fetch the earl. Baker eyed the salmon colored marble walls. The lush carpets with designs and patterns and color schemes unfamiliar with the residents of Fartherland.

Baker glanced up at the Earl as he slowly yet with deliberate stride descended the wide marble staircase. He was of middle-age, tall, rather handsome with a slight belly. He was not dressed in the colorful fare of most of the citizens of the island city. Baker sensed by the way he carried himself that the earl was a man of reason, someone who not merely received his position because of birth but was worthy of his place.

The earl recognized the regalia of the palace guard and knew whatever reason the young man was here for, it was important. "Good day, my good sir," the earl said. "It is rare we see a guard from the royal palace, the king's trusted elite here in Driftwood, never mind at the doorstep of the earl. Please enter into the parlor so we can enjoy some privacy."

The earl shut the door behind him. "Please sit," the earl instructed pointing to a chair. Baker saw the chairs were less formal looking and more comfortable than the hard straight back chairs he was accustomed to. Everything about this city seemed to be about ease and reclining, and so he wondered how the earl would take the news.

"I have come down from Edgewood," Baker began, "to warn you of a dire threat upon this lovely city. You will be visited by a fire-breathing dragon!" he declared with emphasis to sound more convincing, but it sounded too forced. Baker waited for laughter or some mocking comment, but there was neither.

"Have you some official word on this...a scroll with Montague's seal to verify what you have said."

Baker was taken by the earl's sense of proper protocol. The earl had asked a reasonable question. Where did this order originate from? Baker decided to tell the truth and thus be totally disregarded and relieved of his duty and responsibility and alas head back to Edgewood where he belonged.

"A prophet, my lord...the report came from a prophet."

"From the priesthood in The Great City?"

"No, this prophet was not associated with the gods of the Realm. This god the prophet served is also a king and reigns from Mt. Forever."

"I have heard of kings who thought they were gods, but not gods who thought they were kings - an interesting reversal."

"Yes, my lord," was all Baker could think to say.

"Did the prophet tell you why this city would be attacked?"

Another insightful question, Baker thought. "No reason was given."

The earl put his left hand beneath his chin and deep in thought got off the chair and ambled over to a window which looked out over the large square. Baker remained seated and waited for a swift dismissal when suddenly the earl swung around and looking directly at him, asked, "Why do you think this will happen to this city."

"My lord, does a dragon need a reason to attack a city?"

"You are unaware of this place. It not only is a city that is an island in a river. It is an island in the world. It has chosen to cut itself off from the affairs of people. It's only concern with the world is the goods it can export and what it can take in. With all its wealth it turns its back on the seaport of Seven as it falls in upon itself. It abuses its slaves. It has become fat and lazy. They see me as a figurehead. It is the Merchant's Guild that controls the city. They are pleased with me for doing nothing and staying out of the affairs of Driftwood, but I'm tired of it."

The earl was suddenly quiet. Baker waited for him to continue, but he stood looking out the window in silence. It was becoming awkward. Baker finally spoke, "So what are you going to do my lord?"

He turned. "I'm leaving Driftwood."

"And abandon your people?" Baker questioned flummoxed by this man who he thought embraced integrity.

"These are not my people. They are people of the merchant's guild. This city is being judged for its narcissistic behavior."

"But, my lord, what knowledge would a dragon have of such things."

"None, but this prophet of this White King would know of such things. This warning would go unheeded by these people. I have not a few chests of precious jewels and gold and silver. I will reward you well if you accompany me to a city named Splendor along the Beautiful River which divides Westerland from Riverland."

"In accordance with the words of the prophet I must remain in Driftwood."

"Ah, so you have been called to a greater purpose, and I would prevent you from fulfilling your purpose if I was here."

"My lord you cannot be sure of that."

"No, but I can be sure of this. I am leaving. Will you assist me with my treasure down to one of the ships I frequent when I have business away. The merchant guild won't suspect anything or care."

"Of course, my lord."

"I will inform the duke that you will be residing in one of the guest rooms."

"Then I should warn him."

"What did the prophet say?"

"Warn the earl."

"You have done so. The duke is nothing more than a lap dog for the Merchant's Guild. Stay down below in a room beneath the palace during the attack. After which, you can fulfill your destiny here in Driftwood, whatever that may be."

"I am afraid my lord of what may lie ahead for me."

"Take heart Baker of the palace guard. You have either been spoken to by a prophet or a madman. Soon you will learn which one."

Three trips were made carrying three trunks weighed down with precious coins from the palace of the earl to his ship. Baker bowed in respect at the conclusion of his errand. The earl held out a small sack filled with coins. Baker's eyes opened wide. "My lord, this is not necessary."

"Do not be hasty to judge young knight. It may indeed come to be necessary."

"Of course, my lord I will accept, but I wish you were staying."

"You have your destiny to fulfill and I have mine."

The earl boarded the ship and disappeared into a cabin. Baker turned and started back to the palace. With the absence of the earl Baker suddenly felt an awesome responsibility and burden for the city. According to the earl, the duke could not be trusted to take to heart an attack from a dragon, so he concocted another scenario the duke might take seriously and heed.

Baker found the duke at his breakfast table joined by whom Baker assumed to be three of the more wealthy vendors of expensive luxury goods. The duke was not pleased with the knight's interruption. Unlike the earl, the duke was dressed in the colorful and gay garb of the city. He was the opposite character of the earl, embracing his puppet status under the thumb of the merchant guild with comfort and ease.

"My lord, I apologize for my barging in like this on your delicate and sensitive meeting with such distinguished men of your city, but I have been sent here to warn you of a possible attack from the Barman's to our east. It may never come to pass, but your city is vital to the northern territories of the Realm and needs to be defended. You must make ready your knights in the event that such an attack materializes."

Baker noticed the fear and agitation of the three visitors, though the duke seemed oblivious to any real danger. With a flamboyant wave of his hand the duke dismissed Baker, saying, "Do what you must to make our city safe."

"Wait," ordered one of the merchants, "come here young knight." Baker walked over and bowed. The merchant looked at Baker, sizing him up before speaking as if he was examining a piece of merchandise to price out at an exorbitant fare the upper echelon would be willing to pay for yet another unwarranted item into their pretentious lives.

"Young man, you are a palace guard well trained and physically fit. The knights of Driftwood were once dependable polished warriors. Now you will find them out of shape, belligerent, and lazy." The man pulled out a small bag of coins from his satchel. "We have a weapons maker on Bell End. They specialize in arrows of the finest quality. Arrows are our best defense against rowers attacking our walled city. Take these coins and buy what you need for our knights. If you need more, see the duke. He will accommodate."

Baker noticed the irate sideways glance the duke gave the merchant, and answered reluctantly, "Yes, my lords, and I will mention to our king of your gracious aid you have given to the knights of the Realm."

"That would be good," the merchant said and smiled, always pleased to have earned a future favor from the royal palace.

*

Baker ordered the arrows from a guild on Bell End. Then he went to gather the knights of Driftwood. They were rusty from a sedentary life and had become a reflection of the folks they were to defend: lethargic, lazy yet greedy for gain.

At the close of the second day Baker was at wits end with these next to useless knights, until he remembered what the influential merchant had told him that the duke would provide additional financial assistance if needed, and so he spoke with earnest to the reluctant warriors.

"The duke is not pleased with your progress, so he instructed me to tell you something in which you are to share with no one. If so, it will cost you dearly, but if you refrain from saying anything to anyone, you will profit. Your duke has received a rumor that a dragon will attack the city within a week."

Chuckles and an interruption ensued. A large man with

a jutting jaw stepped forward, looked at the men to his left and to his right, and then back at Baker, and announced with confidence, "I speak for us all. We will bring down this dragon for our duke."

Baker stepped back suddenly when the big man bent over with his hands pressed against his knees and roared in laughter. The other knights joined in at the ridiculous command. Another knight who had grown round in the middle, cried out, "We will train for this attack down at the Lazy Man Tavern!" The other men cheered in agreement.

Baker saw the wisdom in playing along with the men, and spoke out, "You and I know that dragons do not exist, but your duke is superstitious. He is frightened, and he has agreed to triple all of your wages. The duke told me that if you men train and prepare yourself for such an attack with rigor and determination that after a fortnight, even if one never comes, you will receive your promised wages."

The knights of Driftwood all glanced at each other in surprise and delight. The man who spoke out first with the jaw that jut out like a granite overhang, spoke again for all the men, "We will do as we are told. We will say nothing, but the gods help you palace guard if we do not receive our promised pay."

A short man pushed his way through the crowd of approximately 70 knights. "My lord, those folks who dwell by the Pale Forest believe in dragons and dragon lore teach that the dragon's weakness is in their filmy thin wings, which if pierced with enough arrows, would plummet the beast from the sky. Thus we should train as archers, convincing our duke of our seriousness to defend the city against a dragon."

"Then archers you will become," Baker said.

*

Two days passed and the knights were excited about their forthcoming extra monies for merely exercising and archery practice. They followed Baker's regiment without complaining, for they had no delusion that a dragon would actually appear. In spite of their laughter and mocking imitations of their ostentatious duke, Baker was pleased with the progress. Their skills recessed beneath a couple years of neglect were now returning, but now it was not so much a lack of ability that concerned him but the opportunity to pierce the wings with enough arrows to bring it down. How many deaths would ensue before the dragon was shot out of the sky, if indeed they could get close enough to do it.

16
An Accusation

Fairhaven who required no sleep rowed through the night and the next day and again through the next evening. His passengers rubbed the sleep from their eyes when they awoke to a scene of wonder and astonishment as they gazed at the high marbled wall of Driftwood looming out of the water.

The city of Seven along the eastern shore of the river appeared dismally rundown juxtaposed against the island city. Fairhaven spoke sadly of its former glory as they sailed past the white circular wall of Driftwood towards Seven to drop off his two passengers: the Lady Kettery and Ursula.

Fairhaven began: "Seven was once the pride of Glendyland. Two centuries ago the island city of Driftwood was carried into the mouth of the River Green. Since then the commerce has been shifting to Driftwood. The citizens of Seven took lightly these denizens from southern shores, but they were not to be made light of. They were quite adroit in the affairs of mercantilism and with their creative skills and ingenuity they began to surpass their competition, and Seven has never been able to gain what it had lost. The city has been able to hang on but as you can see from the condition of its dwellings, just barely."

"It does not look welcoming," Lady Kettery said a little nervous about making this journey to Castle Calamitous without the accompaniment of a man. She looked at Driscoll in desperation. "Driscoll, will you please reconsider?"

"My lady," Fairhaven interrupted, "it is you who should reconsider. You are not prepared to face what awaits you in Castle Calamitous."

"And what will become of Beth? Do we let her languish in that place?"

"It is not her survival I am concerned about, my lady, it is yours."

"If you are so concerned then come with us. We saw what you could do on that river diverting one hundred foot tall trees with barely a push."

"My lady, Beth will not be forgotten or abandoned by the White King."

"It certainly looks that way!"

"My lady, you need not understand but trust."

"I cannot."

"If that be the case, there is a man in Seven who goes by the title the Earl of Devon, though he is not really an earl nor is he from Devon. You will find him, day or night, at a tavern known as The Earl."

"He sounds totally unreliable. Could you not do any better?"

"If the White King could do better, he would."

"I thought this White King wants me to go Driftwood."

"Even in your rebellion he provides what is best."

"I would think he would lead me to a knight and not some drunkard."

"A knight would be better trained but not more committed to your success."

"And this drunkard will be."

"Judge for yourself my lady."

"Please supply someone else."

"You will have to do that yourself because the Earl of Devon has been provided."

Ursula listened to all this and it amazed her. *This Earl who seems totally useless to offer any kind of assistance is the one the White King has provided, the same one who provided Fairhaven. If so, then somehow, this Earl of Devon can be counted on.*

*

"Cowards, they all are…panicked stricken girls, they are. The first word of danger and off they goes Donald."

"I agree," Barda, "no stamina for real life on the borders of the wild."

Suddenly a screech came shooting downriver as the two men, who casually stood on the docks of Wilderwood, looked up to see a giant flying lizard open its fell mouth and with a quick hot burst set the two men aflame. Screaming, they jumped into the river. An eruption of flames exploded along the length of the streets as the fair homes of Wilderwood burned brightly, though the city was nearly empty. The dragon then departed leaving Wilderwood to burn; its vengeance not quenched nor would be until the boy in the boat was destroyed.

Harbinger, Daria, John and Quayfear hid in the dense entanglement along the shore just above Riverwood. "Where do you think it's going," John wondered aloud as they saw the giant creature soar by as it followed the River Green south?

Harbinger speculated: "It is going to the mouth of the river to wait for us."

"We'll never get by it unseen," Quayfear initiated.

"No, we won't but others will. The dragon will not burn every boat that floats by but will wait in hiding until it sees us and then strike. We need a boat the dragon will not recognize. We can barter in Riverwood."

When they arrived, they noticed the docks along the river were nearly empty as word of the dragon spread through the river port town and speculation was that it would return. Dragon lore was adamant that once a dragon was spotted none may live to tell the tale. That was why, it was said that, there were so many legends and very few actual sightings.

"Hello, my good sir we want to bargain," said Harbinger to a quiet muscular man who remained on the docks working on his boat. He had not witnessed the dragon nor any other in all his days and was unconcerned about such trifles.

"The strapping man looked up, and simply said, "With what?"

"Our boat."

The fisherman slowly sauntered over to it. He stood on the creaky wooden boards of the weathered gray platform and glared down at it. He said nothing, just stared at the boat as if some great mystery lie within its very boards. He finally turned his head slowly towards Harbinger in a sloth-like manner, and asked quietly, almost imperceptibly, "What do you want for it?"

"Passage to Seven, that is all."

"Passage to Driftwood and that is all. I can get double the money for my catch in Driftwood."

"Then drop us off in Seven and then go to Driftwood to sell your fish."

"It is not that simple. The fishermen of seven will beat me and steal my catch if I do not accept their pittance of a price. I will take you to Driftwood. It should not be difficult for you to succor passage to Seven. It is little more than two stones throws away from the marble walls."

Harbinger nodded and spoke, "Then the skiff is yours."

The four cramped together below deck – out of sight.

*

It was about midmorning when Merrill, and his two remaining palace guards Kai and Ewar, and Kingsley from Fartherwood arrived at the place where they first put up their boats and from there had journeyed upriver on foot.

"One of the boats is missing," Ewar said, "perhaps Franklin and the boy."

"We have more pressing issues than those two, if it is those two who absconded our boat. We must make haste. Now that we travel by boat maybe we can out distance the dragon," Merrill responded, "and arrive at the fortress before it does."

By the end of day the broken walls of Edgewood came into view as Ewar and Kingsley paddled the last stretch of the river. Kai looked on in disbelief as the view of broken walls magnified with intensity the closer they drew near.

"Look," Kingsley moaned, "the castle was as a plaything to that beast."

Ewar was for once silent without any sarcasm or criticism as he looked on at the incredible destruction.

The four men docked the boat. The village was burned and flattened. They ran up the incline. They climbed over the rubble where the gate once stood and surveyed the devastation of the formidable beast, still at large somewhere they determined. They witnessed a few folks from the hamlet and those knights who miraculously remained unscathed tending to the wounded or carrying the dead outside of the walls to be buried.

An elderly man approached them as they stood in dismay of the desolation before them, and spoke up, "My lord, I can see you are from the guard who were sent out earlier by the emissary and that you ran into some trouble along the way because only four of you have returned."

"Yes," said Merrill, "from a dragon such as this one that has caused this wreckage."

"I have some bad news for you my lord. Our emissary is dead."

Merrill looked on in shock. It had not occurred to him that his master would not have survived, but as he gazed around at the razing of the northern wall the reality of indiscriminate death came to light. He glanced at the others who lowered their head in dismay.

"The news I have gets worse my lord. Our emissary was hurt by falling debris but was not killed. It was at that moment a man ran up to our wounded emissary who I assumed intended to aid him, but instead the stranger quickly glanced around to make sure that no one was looking. In the chaos everyone was fending for themselves and so at an opportune time this man plunged his sword into the chest of the emissary.

"It was then that he noticed I had witnessed the whole thing. He panicked and ran leaving his sword buried inside of the emissary. I retrieved it hoping someone could recognize it.

I don't know who the man was, though he was not from the village below. I know everyone there, nor was he dressed as a knight of Edgewood."

"Who would do such a thing," Ewar raged as they walked along amidst the rubble following the elderly man to the place where the sword was hid.

Kai infuriated, added, "What motivation would anyone here have for murdering the emissary."

The squatty old man led them into a stone lean-to structure in which cut and split fire wood was stacked. He removed the sword he had hidden away. The tip was covered with dry blood. "This is the sword the old man said. It belonged to a young man, rather striking in appearance."

"It does not look familiar," Merrill stated and looked at the others. Kai and Ewar shook their head. Kingsley spoke up. "It is Harbinger's...but why?"

Ewar slid out his sword. "Isn't it obvious? Page discovered the truth. It was indeed you who killed the knights of Dogwood!" Kai also slid out his sword.

"I am innocent!" retorted Kingsley.

"Then why didn't you try to stop him?" Ewar blasted back. "I have heard of your exemplary swordsmanship."

Merrill interrupted. "Wait, Ewar," and then turning to Kingsley, he spoke, "You have been a valuable asset turning the others in, and if you say to me that Harbinger acted alone in this barbarous deed against Baron Durkel's knights, so be it, and the four of us will track Harbinger down together and kill him!"

Kingsley glanced at Harbinger's sword the old man held, and thought: *The emissary must have come to the erroneous conclusion that it was me and Harbinger who killed those knights. But now I have an opportunity to remove myself from any future accusations by blaming this matter solely on Harbinger, who has now forfeited any hope of redemption anyway by murdering the emissary. It will not ease, lighten, or change Harbinger's situation by arguing that he did not kill the Baron's knights.*

"It is as you say my lord. Harbinger acted alone." Kingsley then turned to Ewar. "I was shocked at Harbinger's brutal attack. Perhaps I should have responded, but I was afraid and had always been intimidated by my friend. I confess I behaved cowardly but have been attempting to make up for my previous hesitation by doing the honorable thing now."

Merrill stated, "We all have been in frightening situations and had moments of weakness and regrets. Kingsley you have proven worthy of a second chance, and you shall get it."

Kai, who had remained silent, was reminded of his cowardly behavior during the assault of the dragon upon their bivouac and spoke up, "I agree. We all have had moments of indecision."

"The matter is settled." Merrill then stated with authority. "We will perform a proper burial tomorrow morning for the emissary. After which, the four of us start out in pursuit of the miscreant."

Ewar was unconvinced but said nothing.

Merrill then turned to the old man. "Sir, your name – after Harbinger is apprehended and killed, I will send a guard here to amply reward you for your aid."

"That is most generous of you my lord. My name is Banebreath."

17

The Seedy Side of Seven

Fairhaven pushed off from the pier, leaving Ursula and Lady Kettery standing alone like a couple of forlorn pets dropped off where there was little chance of survival. Lady Kettery looked around at the dingy tilted structures along the shore of the Midland Sea built upon old gray pilings. Little upkeep had been done over the years as if the intention was to suck out as much life as they could from these building until they become so dilapidated they collapse in upon themselves, and the folks simply pack up and move down to the city of Six and repeat, as if they were a spreading virus. And in the eyes of Lady Kettery that is all the city folk appeared to resemble.

She took great comfort in the four pieces of silver worth 100 quib Fairhaven had given to her. He had told her it was for victuals and stays, but she was thinking more in line of a mercenary to guide them to Castle Calamitous.

One thing they had going for them was their road-worn look. Their disheveled hair and dirty clothes had them fitting right in with the average folk here. No one gave them a second glance.

"Our first order of business," Lady Kettery said while giving a distrusting eye along the streets of Seven, "is to get ourselves some food, and then find a worthy knight who will guide us to the castle."

"My lady, I think you should reconsider. Fairhaven got us here safely. Perhaps we should trust him and at least give this Earl of Devon a chance."

Lady Kettery's deep seated response of defiance had been somewhat cooled of late, and she actually gave it a moment's thought. "We will inquire within the tavern Fairhaven mentioned called 'The Earl.' After which, we will have no more talk about it."

They saw a sign of a local tavern ahead. The paint was half flaked off but upon closer examination it read, The Earl. It was a shanty looking establishment. Lady Kettery peered inside. "This is your doing, not mine Ursula. I wish you the best."

The door opened and a tall man stumbled out.

"Excuse me sir," Ursula said, "do you know of a man known as the Earl of Devon."

He mumbled some kind of curse at the mention of the title "Earl" and then slurred his words, "He's inside." Ursula looked on as the tall man with torn breeches and soiled jerkin made a feeble attempt at walking in a normal cadence down the road. She was now beginning to have doubts about this earl herself. Ursula glanced fitfully back inside the shadowy room where light was a rare commodity. She turned to her mistress with uncertainty but said nothing.

"If he is in no better condition than that man!" blasted Lady Kettery, "I don't want him…understood?"

Ursula opened the creaky door. A few grubby dock workers and an array of weary forgotten men turned to see the latest hard pressed cohort walk into the dingy place. Some bore gray and black spiked whiskers; others peered at the maiden amidst long strands of stringy hair dangling in front of bloodshot eyes, and others with thick wiry beards framed mouths with missing teeth, all of which heartily approved of the visage before them. Ursula closed the door and looked at her lady. "Your way is best."

"Of course my way is best, but you must learn to finish what you started. It is how you move forward in this world. Observe and learn." Lady Kettery opened the door, stepped over the threshold into the gloomy dark walled room, and shouted. "We are looking for the Earl of Devon. Please step outside," she ordered in her demanding way. She then glanced over at Ursula. "You must learn to take charge. They are frightening looking, but they are useless. That is why they are here. That is why this will not work, but you must learn this for yourself."

A hefty man sauntered from around the bar. He did not swagger as the previous man did. His face was wide, his white hair combed back, and he sported a neatly trimmed white beard and mustache. As he approached the sunlit area near the entrance Lady Kettery saw that his eyes were kind. Then her jaw dropped. "It cannot be…it cannot be!" she gasped.

Ursula looked at her oddly. "You know him?"

"I…I don't know…not sure."

The man dressed in a loose brown shirt with tight light beige pants stepped outside. "May I be of assistance ladies?" he asked rather expressionless.

"Are you him…you are him. What is your name?"

"Charles."

"Do you know who I am?"

"Yes, my lady."

Finally Ursula had enough of this clandestine talk. "Who is he?"

"He is the father of Beth," she said in a straight forward manner.

Ursula, unsure of proper protocol when a greeting a man who had had an illicit affair years ago with her upstanding lady of the community, simply bowed and said, "My lord."

"You may call me Charles. I am not your lord or anyone else's lord." The stout looking man then turned to Lady Kettery, saying, "You look well, my lady."

She looked at him and then glanced around the dirty tavern with disdain, and said, "You're the same but for some extra poundage."

"What brings you to our fair city," he asked facetiously, his arm extended in a welcoming motion toward the rundown buildings.

"The place suits you Charles. I am not surprised to see you here. The false appellation: the Earl of Devon is to signify what…lost aspirations – oh no, pardon me, no aspirations."

"And why do you boast since your aspirations have brought you here. Lowering your standards in your old age, my lady?"

Ursula was amazed at this bickering dialogue. They share a daughter taken by some kind of witch, have not seen each other in years, and the best they can do is joust barbs at each other.

Lady Kettery could see Ursula was not impressed at their childish antics, and broke out, "May we get down to business Charles. It is a long story, but it comes down to this: Beth has been taken by some kind of witch and has been absconded to Castle Calamitous. My servant and I are going to rescue her, but we need a guide."

Charles' cheerful playful countenance lost all joviality. He raised his right hand and began stroking his beard, lost in thought. He finally spoke. "So you have come here for my assistance?"

"We came here because we were told by someone that the Earl of Devon could be counted on. Apparently he does not know you as well as I do."

"Apparently he does. I will assist you of course, my lady, for Beth's sake. It is an evil place you speak of. It is located on Mount Odious. It is surrounded by the Pale Forest. Its inhabitants are warlocks and witches, and I have been told, harpies. No offense to this lovely maiden but couldn't you have brought along some young manly servants to assist you?"

"There was one man who traveled with us, but he turned out to be more useless than you."

Ursula bristled up. "My lady," she pronounced, "is it not obvious that Fairhaven guided you here for a reason."

"To show us his humor or lack of judgment perhaps!"

"Your servant is wise, my lady. We must set aside our arguing for the sake of Beth."

Lady Kettery said in a huff, "She is not wise…but she is loyal and I am glad she is here." Lady Kettery glanced over and acknowledged her approval with a nod for insisting they stop quarreling and tend to what had to be done.

She looked at Charles, and spoke forthrightly, "Ursula and I will buy some new clothes conducive for traveling, bathe, and find a clean inn if one exists here."

"I recommend the Carousel. I will pick you up in the morning."

Lady Kettery and Ursula started down the rut lined road. Ursula was pleased with Charles. *This unexpected turn in my lady's life will work out for my benefit. My lady is with her former lover and they will unite for now if only for their daughter. In turn their love, if it still exists, which probably does since the arguing has revealed pride rather than anger, will bind them together and then along with Beth they will be a family. My future will be more secure with both of them rather than with just her. I have to make this work.*

*

Fairhaven docked at Driftwood with Driscoll and led him through the main gate. Driscoll had only heard of the opulence of this city but was now amazed at what he saw, the tall marble structures and the well-dressed men and woman ambling down the well maintained streets.

The two walked on until they came to a tavern called The High House that was like no other tavern Driscoll had ever seen, nor were the clientele typical tavern loiterers. The two men stepped inside. Their raiment was out of place and initially received some disdainful glares, but as Fairhaven scanned the room, the customers slowly returned to their food and paid no attention to the two dirty and frazzled visitors.

Driscoll noticed that the paneled walls were neither of pine nor any native wood of Fartherland. It had a slight purple color to it; and these were no hastily built rickety trestle tables but solid round tables of varying sizes made of some kind of rich black wood. Finally, Driscoll said, "What are we doing here, my lord?"

"You need employment in this city. The White King has seen fit to establish you here."

"I can see he is a benevolent king."

"It is good you see it that way, Driscoll, because he is; though there are those who think he is careless and unsympathetic, but it is because they do not see the whole picture but only its part."

"I like what I see, my lord, in whole and in part."

"I know the proprietor is looking for help in the kitchen. Let us find the owner. His name is Tumbrel." Fairhaven led Driscoll to the back of the tavern where the servants worked in a well apportioned room. Driscoll was impressed with the tidiness of it and the quality of its help. Young men and women scurried about, though not in a chaotic fashion but in a timely and efficient manner. Driscoll smiled to himself. How he will enjoy having such servants under him. The Kettery manor was a step above The Corner Tavern, but this was a big step above that. This employment was more than anybody of his social status could imagine.

Fairhaven addressed a middle age man of average build and height and said, "I have been told you need another worker in the scullery. I have just the man. His name is Driscoll."

Tumbrel gave the filthy looking man a quick glance, and spoke, "His appearance will suit his position." Driscoll smiled proudly. "Wait here," Tumbrel commanded.

"I am in your debt, my lord, for such an opportunity as this," Driscoll said humbly to Fairhaven.

"Not my debt but the King's."

"Of course, my lord."

"Do not lose heart Driscoll - this is not your final destination."

"What do you mean not lose heart...what do you mean not my final destination?"

Just then Tumbrel returned with a younger man in tow. He spoke directly to Driscoll. "I have two other such taverns in Driftwood. I manage the largest one in the Square. My son, John, runs this one."

"John...his name is John."

"Yes," the young man said, "and you Driscoll will be given the most base and menial work in the place." It is a position which takes stamina and fortitude, but primarily it takes someone desperate enough to take on such cruel labor. Your appearance speaks of your desperation. John then chuckled loudly. "You start immediately. Follow me."

"Wait one moment!" Driscoll turned to address Fairhaven, but he was gone. Driscoll reached in his pockets and felt around. He carried not even a half quib to his name. He was as desperate as he looked.

John turned around. "Come now Driscoll. There is no one else in this city who will hire you except those who work amidst the smelly filth of the canal. You are much better off here. Consider yourself blessed by the gods!" John exclaimed and laughed aloud at the pathetic large man who followed behind.

18

THE UNSUSPECTING CITY

Banebreath and the dragon waited in hiding in the deep green boughs of the evergreens. Banebreath assumed that Harbinger and his companions would transfer to a boat he wouldn't recognize, believing they could slip by him unnoticed and warn the people of Driftwood. But unbeknownst to them the scent of John who had killed the infant dragon was forever etched in the memory of the mother.

It was late afternoon when Banebreath noticed the dragon whose head lay on the ground suddenly stir, its nostrils flaring. John was near! Banebreath crawled through the undergrowth to the water's edge and saw a fishing boat circling the wall, heading for the main gate along the southern perimeter. It was time!

Daria led Harbinger, John, and Quayfear into a city which did not carry pleasant memories. The other three swiveled their heads taking in the affluence and finery of the place. Daria noticed their gawkish expressions, and said, "Do not think we will be welcomed here. We will not."

Harbinger shook his head. "We have no monies and nothing to barter with."

"We need only to get to the shore of Glendyland in order to begin our pilgrimage to The Great City," said Quayfear. "Surely there should be someone who would oblige us free passage to the city of Seven. It is very close."

"It is our only hope," Harbinger said in agreement as he looked around at those passing by who took no notice of them. It was as if they were invisible. "Daria is right. There is no help for us inside these walls. Let us search the docks in hope for some passage across the river."

Daria joined Quayfear and searched the West side of the dock facing Fartherland. They had inquired with three small vessels, but there was no interest in doing anything gratis. 'No quib, no ride' was all they heard.

Quayfear was taken by the seagulls perched on the tall piles, hoping for any scraps of food discarded by merchants throwing away inferior imports not measuring up to the finicky tastes of their customers, when suddenly all of them simultaneously, whether by telepathy or whether no communication was needed, flew towards the mainland squawking loudly. Quayfear turned towards Daria. "Something is wrong. What do you see?"

Daria was also taken aback by the sudden rush of white and gray wings. The sudden blast of high pitch caws from the harbor scavengers left Daria unable to hear what Quayfear had said. In the distance she noticed some movement along the Fartherland shore. In her head she heard a voice: 'Go to building number six in the square of the city...now!' She could not make out the image among the conifers along the banks of the river but she knew, she knew it was there...the dragon!

Daria without warning ran back towards the gate of the city. Quayfear turned and shouted, "Where are you going?"

"Luck is not with us," said Harbinger to John after they exhausted all their resources on the eastern side of the wharf. "Let's find Daria and Quayfear." They turned and started back towards the main gate.

The flight of the seagulls had captured the attention of all those along the great circular wharf, though no one could make out the reason for the exodus. With the birds gone there was suddenly an eerie quietness as if the whole world had stopped. Quayfear stood alone sensing something. Even the wind had ceased. "Oh no," he verbalized, "it's here!"

Banebreath pierced the mind of the dragon. The behemoth creature stirred from its frozen position in the pines. The duke's death was to be the first, to set an example of the fate of the whole city. This display would strike utter fear, hopelessness, and resignation in the people.

The brutish thing lumbered to the side of the river and glanced at the island city. The beast did not like flying so close to the white marbled wall, but every indication revealed the city was unsuspecting of anything out of the ordinary. The ramparts were empty. They had not heard of the destruction up north. It was safe to fly.

The black beast stood on its hind legs on the bank of the river; the soft earth settled without resistance under the enormous weight of the creature, leaving two large imprints. The dragon slowly raised two sprawling wings. As if on silent hinges the appendages splayed out while a frightening shadow fell over the passing current. The dragon raised its massive wings high and with a great force downward the wings broke the calm air around it, stirred up a wind that blew across the water causing it to ripple as the beast lifted itself from the earth and into the sky.

It only took a few moments for the men on the piers to notice the flying reptile, and moments later panic ensued. Everyone on mass started towards the gate. The dragon ignored them and flew towards the duke's palace.

The duke heard the commotion outside his balcony facing the river and went out to check on the situation. Below him he saw men scrambling towards the gate...*what for?* The duke then noticed a blanket of grayness overshadow him. He glanced up and saw the dragon's huge head descending upon him. He screamed and tripped running for the door.

The young duke felt the jaws of the flying creature clasp his ankle, and he was lifted off the floor of the marbled balcony Dangling from the mouth of the dragon, the leathery winged creature now flew over the city revealing its taste for live flesh. Those inside the circular walls screamed while glancing up at the spectacle.

The duke's head faced downward as he hung limply, his left foot wedged between two of the dragon's teeth. His anger flared as he saw the people far below staring up and pointing as if he was on display. He cursed aloud, "Help me you useless imbeciles! I hate you...always have, always will! I call down anathema on you!"

"What is he saying?" one woman asked.

"He must be telling us to run for shelter, come!"

The dragon bent its head forward and snapping her neck up suddenly, it let go of the duke as he flipped over and over several times in the air as if part of an act in a minstrel show. As soon as the duke's body could sail no farther up it began to plummet. In a few dizzying glimpses the helpless liege noticed the giant animal flying upward towards him, its cavernous mouth opened wide. The duke landed on a soft slimy tongue which acted like a large chute.

He screeched a blood curdling cry as he dug his fingers into the slippery surface covered with gooey saliva. He began sliding down the greasy tongue towards the black tunnel before him. He tumbled and rolled down the dark throat, when suddenly a bright light emerged from below. The duke felt the heat, at first comfortable but then unbearable as a searing flame engulfed him and sent him flying out of the mouth of the dragon.

Those on the ground marveled at the ball of fire but as the flame disappeared a small black figure shot across the sky. The charred body smashed against one of the building in the square and fell onto the pavers below. The burnt man lay on his back, mouth open, its eyes burnt out of their sockets. A woman screamed, looked up, and noticed the dragon descending upon their city.

It flew down and landed on the roof of the Duke's palace. It noticed Daria in the square, and their eyes met. She noticed the number six etched upon the door. The dragon waited until Daria ran inside. Then it began its attack.

The creature swung her head from left to right, letting out a sweeping flame of fire running along the floor of the great square below. Numerous people burst into flames. Screaming in agony they resembled moving torches running into each other with no one who could help quench the pain of burning flesh.

Harbinger and John were spared the dragon's first round as they tried running for shelter in one of the buildings along the periphery of the square. The dark beast caught a glimpse of John, the one who murdered her baby. The dragon in a rage flew down and landed in the square amongst the frightened people. It took one of its wings and dragged it like a broom across the pavers, sweeping a pile of screeching humans towards its large elongated head, hoping to pluck John out of the stack of fleshly debris to slowly chew on him, its serrated teeth crushing and breaking his bones with each crunch while the boy would cry in agony without any relief.

Men, women, and children scraped and cut screamed in horror as the large face with piercing eyes studied the pile of human flesh it had gathered with its wing. Its keen eye caught the boy from Fartherwood. In that instant John recalled the words of Dresler from the meeting in the wilderness. 'You must find a sword in Edgewood. You will need it.' *But how can this sword or any sword make any difference against plates of iron.*

Suddenly John realized that Franklin's old rusty sword that he found behind the tavern wasn't special nor was Franklin special, but the White King is; and Franklin believed in him. It was trust and faith in what Franklin could not see that enabled the sword.

John crawled beneath the bodies piled on one another. The dragon could have burned them all alive but that would be too quick a death for the boy. He had to suffer. The dragon spread its left wing that enveloped the people into a heap and let the pathetic frightened people, who were able, to scurry away so as to get a glimpse of the boy. Out of the corner of its sinister eye it saw the lad standing along its right side where its other wing was clasped tightly against its black scales.

John took his sword and thrust it through the thin sensitive webbing and the blade easily pierced through the rock solid plates. John forced the blade in up to the hilt and let go leaving the sword buried in the beast, its right wing pinned against its side. The monster let out a wretched cry and with all its power and muscle could not free the pinned wing. The blade held fast.

At that moment Baker led the knights from another part of the city into the North end of the square after hearing the commotion. He hesitantly glanced around almost hoping to see Page stepping out from amongst the crowd with that confident look, an assurance he naturally projected that no matter what was happening you sensed a calmness which exuded from his presence. He was an endearing leader, but he was gone.

Baker looked over at the knights who were in the position he envied, simply waiting for a command. The weight of success or failure fell upon him, and he felt the burden which was now his.

The beast saw John running towards the knights of Driftwood for protection. In a great rage the beast pounded towards the knights, its heavy feet crushing anyone or anything in its path. With its free wing now safely folded along its side, the knights had no target in which the arrows could have an effect. Baker saw many of the knights with a look of doom on their faces drop their bows and run.

"Hold your ground!" Baker shouted at the thirty knights who remained.

"We have no target, my lord!"

"You will! Fifteen of you line up in front. Release your arrows when I say. They will be useless against the hardened exterior, but it will incite the dragon to open its mouth. Then kneel down and let the men who stand behind you fire their arrows into the widening jaws of insatiable wreckage. Then the first fifteen stand up and shoot again into the dark void, the pit of blackness and fire; then kneel and the others let go another round into the ravenous hollow. In doing so the dragon will gag, thus putting the fire out!"

The thirty knights strung their bows and waited, their arms shaking at the sight of the deadly beast drawing near to them. They could feel their hearts pounding against their ribs.

The black monster stopped in front of the array of knights, staring at the men, unnerving them to shoot their arrows and waste them upon its hard scalloped plates in which they would merely bounce off.

"Do not fire your arrows!" Baker shouted, "Until I give the command." The arms of the men shook as their muscles strained to keep from letting their arrows fly. Finally the command came and in great relief the front line of men released their fingers from the arrows and they shot forward in a whiz splintering upon hitting the rock-like plates.

Thinking that all the men had released their arrows the dragon felt safe enough now to open its mouth and release a driving force of searing fire that would engulf all thirty knights in one shot. At that moment the men in front knelt down and Baker yelled out, "Shoot!" Those standing behind now fired their arrows into the mouth of the fell creature. Those kneeling stood up and fired another round into the open cavern, immediately knelt and those behind let go another round.

This repeated until the dragon's mouth resembled a pin cushion full of needles. Arrows stuck in its tongue, the roof of its mouth and down into the throat of the animal. It now began to gag. "Again!" Baker yelled.

The dragon realized she had to leave while she could. The colossal creature spread its one wing and lifted itself off the floor of the square, but it struggled with only one working appendage, its other still pinned to its side held firmly by John's sword. It barely managed to clear the wall.

The dragon's wing continued to work furiously but the bulk of the beast shifted to the right as it cleared the ramparts, and the prodigious weight of the monster crashed into the marble wall. The great stone blocks shuddered but held firm. The circular construction had the effect of transferring much of the blow around the rest of the wall; but the force of the falling creature nudged the island which had been anchored to the riverbed for two centuries.

The behemoth lizard fell into the river on its back smashing into fragments the portion of the piers and docks beneath it. The dragon took one last breath before going under. The bulky heavy frame of scales and muscle hit the riverbed stirring up the mucky bottom, muddying up the water. Its long neck shot upward to desperately gasp some fresh air, but the beast found its flaring nostrils three feet below the surface of the river, its forlorn gaze looking up at a blurry blue sky. With dazed eyes its mouth fell open to receive the river. The current mercilessly twisted the long neck and pounded the head cruelly against the roots of the island.

*

Quayfear heard the dock smash to pieces, so he boarded a small abandoned skiff. Between Quayfear's poor eyesight and the cacophony of cries and screams and massive chaos behind the walls, he was left with no other alternative but to wait there for the others to come in search for him, if they were even still alive.

Suddenly he heard cheers thundering upward from behind the walls. Inside the people gathered round their heroes, praising their efforts, but Baker drew their attention and shouted, "People, we can celebrate later. Right now tend to the wounded!"

The wealthy citizens of Driftwood gazed at this young handsome knight, who under impossible odds organized the once slothful knights into a fighting unit. They realized they now heard the voice of someone, the likes of they have not heard in recent memory, someone they could admire, look up to and who the guild could not control, a true leader.

A large burly distinguished older gentlemen with a deep booming voice shouted to the people, "The gods have not been pleased with our greed, our hoarding of wealth; yet some god has sent us this palace guard to save our city. Let us show that god that we were worth rescuing. Let us tend to the wounded as the knight has commanded, lest something worse befalls us."

Many responded to the urgent call, the square was a repulsive scene of burnt corpses. Those trying to assist slipped and slid on slippery cobblestones covered with blood from the screaming wounded and the silent dead. Harbinger could not find John. He looked across the square and saw Daria standing on a second story balcony in full view. His hope was that John saw her too. Harbinger started towards the building.

Daria was appalled by the brutal attack but had already experienced first hand the death and ruination the animal was capable of, but in spite of the pain and suffering it had caused, she pushed it away and focused on the loss of this creature's mystical powers to guide her. Now what would she do. Her only alternative now was to find Harbinger if he was alive, or rather have him find her. She remained on the balcony in plain view of all down below.

It took some time but the three of them were finally reunited at the former duke's palace. "Where is Quayfear?" Harbinger asked in a panic. "He was with you Daria?"

"When I saw the creature, I panicked and ran inside the walls for cover. I am sorry about your little friend," she said without pity or remorse.

"Then you left him outside the walls?"

"Yes," she said, with subtle delight.

"Good, Daria, you have done well. That was the safest place for him."

She bit down on her tongue in hidden rage. He was not angry.

"Let us find him."

The three went out the open gate and found Quayfear in a skiff, joined him, and sailed for the town of Seven along the coast of Glendyland.

As they crossed the mouth of the Green, Harbinger noticed Quayfear turn his gaze upriver. The scribe's thoughts he imagined were not on what they had just been through but on his fellow scribe and friend. Harbinger, too, wondered how Franklin was doing. Did they avoid the dragon? Did they make it to the plains and what or who was there to greet them? There was no way of knowing.

He glanced at Daria whose face was set south towards The Great City as if something awaited her there. Daria seemed more eager than they were to get there, her motivation more urgent, yet where did it come from.

Harbinger was hoping that with the death of the dragon Daria would return back to her previous self, but her frozen stare was fixed, determined to withstand all obstacles and hazards and to arrive at her desired destination.

19

Separated

The ceremonial burial for the emissary was held at sunrise. Knights from the fortress and townsfolk from the village gathered together outside of what was left of the walls of the castle. Merrill spoke of the emissary's past exploits which he had shared alongside his former commander and friend. He concluded with hope and a promise: "The fortress of Edgewood has always been an important and vital defense from our enemies who might find advantage in a strategic offensive by way of the River Green. Upon our return to The Great City we will inform the king to send up stone cutters and wood wrights, blacksmiths and laborers to rebuild."

A roar of cheers arose above the solemn moment. At that the burial ceremony for the emissary ended. Kai did not join in the uproar but looked on in sadness at the emissary's still corpse and recalled Ulric, a palace guard, who was also killed in what they had labelled the quaint hamlet; and now his other traveling companion, Baker, the knight from Dogwood who Page took a liking to, was believed to be among the dead in Edgewood, buried beneath the debris.

That was yesterday but now Merrill, Kai, Ewar, and Kingsley gawked at the total destruction of Wilderwood as they rowed by the burnt homes and taverns; the inns and guilds. Smoke rose from the charred building. The entire city looked like the inside of a smoking caldron, the woods around it left unscathed.

Kai spoke solemnly, "The gods have judged us. We have not done well in their eyes."

"It is possible," Merrill said. "We will enquire with the priesthood upon our return. One thing is certain. We have awoken an evil power."

"The Realm has done nothing to awaken an evil power," said Ewar caustically, "but if anyone has awoken an evil source it was those from Fartherwood. This all began with them."

"Perhaps," sighed Merrill, "but do not think that Kingsley here is one of them. He has been cleared. We have had this discussion Ewar," Merrill concluded forcefully.

"Of course, my lord, present company excluded," Ewar said submissively, biting his tongue.

*

The Island City, which Driftwood was sometimes referred to, was in chaos; but the proprietor of The High House saw it as his primary duty to keep the tavern open so those lost in sorrow and grief could find solace in an expensive glass of imported wine or local mead. This was his burden to bear in shouldering the recovery of disenchanted folks.

Driscoll now stood in the kitchen of his new place of employment. It was an upscale tavern of exquisite taste and charm and except for the brute son of the proprietor it would have suited him well. But his treatment from John, his new master, was wretched and humiliating. He was regarded worse than a dog, yet he was the only one who submitted to the will of the White King and went to Driftwood, and this was the thanks he had gotten!

Driscoll recalled yesterday how the Island City shook when the dragon hit the wall and plummeted into the river and how he had stumbled while balancing a tray of hearty stew. The whole island seemed to have moved from its mooring.

After the jolt, he regained his balance and heard over to his right a crash. He looked to see an expensive artifact on display shatter. He could still hear the proprietor's voice ringing in his ears. "Driscoll, hurry, tend to that shattered vase now!" No sooner had he grabbed a heavily frayed straw broom that he heard his name again, "Driscoll, we have spillage on the kitchen floor. Clean it up now!" Driscoll abandoned his station with the chards of the exquisite vase and ran into the kitchen huffing. He saw John with a sneer pointing at the door, and saying, "Get out there and clean off the tables of those who left in haste."

Driscoll had glared hard at the young man with such hatred it made John want to laugh in joy, and he said, "Is there something wrong slave? With the lack of progress you are making you may be stuck doing menial tasks until you take your last breath."

But now it was early dawn of the following day, and John was not in yet. Driscoll recalled Fairhaven's words. The White King saw it fit for him to remain there for a while and that his situation would change but how long would that take and what was the reason for such underserved treatment – as if he were being punished for something, but he thought to himself...*for what?*

*

Charles knocked upon the door of the room at the inn where Lady Kettery and Ursula had spent the night. Lady Kettery opened it and stood silently before him. He noticed the effort it took for her to stand above the fray, but Charles saw beyond the stiff figure of an aging monument trying to cling to the former bustling aggressive entrepreneur of years ago. Behind the stone façade she was scarred, and all her efforts were spent covering them. He wondered if she ever grew weary of keeping up the facade. He supposed not.

He knew his quiet demeanor and disdain for upper crust formality had not found favor with the ambitious daughter of a thriving merchant. The echelon of dignitaries and royalty that Lady Kettery loved to hobnob with he found barely tolerable. He was a simple man and wanted a simple life. The couple seemed doomed from the start, and it proved to be so.

Charles nature hadn't changed after all these years, though nor had hers. It was good they went separate ways in spite of a daughter they shared. Neither was a romantic but a realist. It made for an equitable parting.

"Are you ready," he asked her.

"Yes, we are."

"I left Gerard in charge of the tavern. I have a wagon I use to cart kegs of ale. I've brought some cushions for the seats. Our journey will take us four to five days depending on the weather. I have brought victuals from my root cellar. We can replenish them along the way."

"Then let us begin," Lady Kettery said, glancing over at Ursula who stood quietly waiting and ready. *She is bolder than I ever imagined, maybe even more than me, but she will never know that.*

*

Harbinger, Quayfear, John, and Daria straggled into Seven. People were involved in their daily routine with one difference. All the talk was of the fallen dragon, for nearly everyone had seen the spectacle.

"What are we going to do?" John asked Harbinger. "We have no coins amongst us."

"I have an idea," Quayfear said.

"Lead the way," Harbinger responded, surprised and impressed to see Quayfear show initiative.

Quayfear had always used his poor eyesight as an excuse to remain in the background to be a tag-along, a follower's follower, but he sensed something changing. For some reason he did not perceive his eyesight as much a hindrance any more – certainly not a benefit, but his purpose could be wrought in spite of it.

Daria gazed at Harbinger oddly for not even questioning the half blind roly-poly scribe as to his intention. She saw Harbinger clearly regressing from the innovative aggressive knight he was in Fartherwood to a mealy submissive jester. Something had happened to him and not for the better, and it was tied to that scroll.

Quayfear saw the sign of a local inn and in a most unusual uncharacteristic manner led them inside. The owner immediately sensed trouble at the sight of these wayfarers. But without saying a word Quayfear strode up to the desk confidently and pulled out the scroll and showed the proprietor the emissary's seal and spoke without hesitation, "We have a message for our king. We have been pursued by the dragon your city witnessed yesterday. We need food, bath, and rooms for the night."

The man quickly glanced down at the royal seal and then up at this seemingly hodgepodge of couriers from the king, and said somewhat hesitantly, "Of course my lords." The man led Quayfear, Harbinger, and John to a large room to share and Daria to a small private one. The four ate well and slept all day and through the night. The following morning they bathed and went down to the docks. They had no money but they were hoping that with the sealed scroll they could also find free passage.

They approached a young sailor appearing ready to depart. Harbinger said, "We are going to the Great City. We have a scr..."

Fairhaven dressed as a seaman interrupted, "You're not going to the Great City - at least not yet. Dresler has so ordered. You are going to make a brief stop first at Castle Calamitous."

With an untrusting gaze Harbinger asked, "You know Dresler...how?"

"I am one of his servants."

"So you say."

"Yes, I do."

There was an awkward silence as Harbinger waited for this stranger to give some kind of proof of his identity, but the stranger stood in silence as if to say, *Can we go on or need we stand here in silence all day.*

Harbinger cleared his throat, and spoke, "John has informed us Dresler is the son of the White King, but what does this White King want with us?"

"He wants you to listen to his son."

"What is our purpose?"

"It will be revealed in due time."

"In due time - in due time!" Daria interrupted in a blind rage. "In due time, Harbinger will be a quivering little boy taking orders from anyone who raises his head to speak! Since you are connected with this White King and Dresler, it is best to bid you farewell here and now...good day," she said stiffly.

She noticed Harbinger turn red in anger and she approved. "Well, at least there is some hope for you yet," she said to him in a condescending tone.

"What has happened to you?" he asked harshly.

"Nothing has happened to me! I am thinking rationally. What has happened to you? You are being led around like a bull with a ring in its nose because of that scroll and some kind of special sword – which is nothing more than some kind of dark power disguised in white."

Daria then turned her attention to Fairhaven. "What do you want from us? What is in this castle you speak of?"

"Beth has been captured by an evil lord from the underworld, a servant of the Prince of Genadar."

"Sandgrit," Quayfear whispered to himself, remembering the conversation the Baron had with Sandgrit prior to his leave of Dogwood.

Fairhaven had no trouble hearing the faintest whisper. "It is not Sandgrit," he corrected. "It is Blackrose, a servant from Lady Kettery's manor."

"Don't be ridiculous," Daria interjected. "Blackrose is a quiet nondescript young wench. She is harmless." She turned to her traveling companions. "This is nothing more than a plot to keep us from King Fenelon."

Harbinger looked at Daria in surprise at her cavalier attitude towards her best friend's imprisonment. "What of Beth?" Harbinger asked amazed at how quickly Daria lost concern for her friend.

Daria glared at Harbinger and then turned towards the newcomer and said, "Why doesn't this White King and his son

Dresler rescue Beth. What can we do against a dark lord of the underworld?"

The three men looked questioningly at Fairhaven in support of Daria's fair inquiry.

Fairhaven responded in an even tone, "You can do nothing against this dark lord alone, but you are not alone. Your special sword will enable you to go against her, though that is not the main problem. Lady Kettery, Ursula, and a man named Charles who is accompanying the two women are on their way to save Beth, but they will be killed without your help."

"No!" said Daria firmly. "How impotent is this one you follow. We should put this White King to the test and see if he can rescue Lady Kettery and Ursula and this man who is with them and prove to us his worth. Perhaps then we might concede that this White King is a force to be reckoned with."

"If you leave now for The Great City, Daria, you will come to learn that he is a force to be reckoned with."

"This situation is not our problem or responsibility," Daria spat back as if she was a personification of the recent dragon they encountered. She looked at Harbinger and Quayfear in a commanding manner and said, "We are wasting time! We need to deliver the message you carry to our king."

Fairhaven ignored the servant girl and approached the four of them, and said, "Here is one hundred Quib. One person should not carry it all in case you get separated." He then handed them each the monies worth twenty-five a piece.

Daria greedily grabbed it and then spoke out to her companions, "We don't even know if this man speaks the truth?"

"Those who bear a special sword know I speak the truth," Fairhaven said. "I have a sword for each of you. You will need it on your journey east." He swung off a long leather tube from off his shoulder and handed each one a sword and scabbard. Then the servant of the White King, without another word, turned and walked away. All of them just stood watching as he walked amongst those along the docks and instantly he blended in so well they could not tell him apart.

"I now hold a special sword," Daria proclaimed, "yet I still do not know whether he speaks the truth or not."

John responded, "The sword is not magical. The barer of the sword does not wield the power either. Its power comes from the White King. This is what I learned from Dresler in the wilderness. You say you do not know if Fairhaven speaks the truth, but I do," John stated proudly.

Daria glanced at the other two.

Harbinger and Quayfear simply nodded.

"This is merely a conspiracy to cajole me into coming along with you. These swords are simply swords."

"Your assessment is correct," John stated. "They are ordinary but can become extraordinary." John glanced down at the scabbard that hung down nearly touching the ground. He then raised his head and his eye caught a piling which extended well above the platform of a pier. Daria was perplexed as she saw the boy stare at the sword and then raise his head and stare at the post and then lower his head and stare at his sword again.

There is nothing special about these swords Daria thought. *What is he doing?*

John stepped toward the piling. He stood before the post and in a flash raised the sword and swung it, slicing off the top eight inches of the pillar.

Daria glanced over at the chunky scribe who watched in amazement that John could now do with that sword what Franklin could do with the one he found behind the tavern. Quayfear instantly recalled a line from the scroll that somehow had eluded him: 'You all shall receive a special sword.'

The scribe stepped forward, brushed away the golden locks which dangled before his eyes and removed the sword from its sheath. The tip of it dropped and hit the planks on the pier. The swords weight was unexpected. He walked over to the post and awkwardly swung the sword cutting another four inches off of it.

Daria noticed that again the sword did not merely nick the post, which would have been the natural effect. She then glared at Harbinger and wondered if he would take his final step into obscurity, settling for a life following fanciful tales of magical swords and secret scrolls.

Harbinger, after just witnessing the power that sword commanded in the hands of two most unlikely swordsmen, wondered: *There was nothing special about Franklin's sword, yet it could split an anvil. There was nothing special about that sword we fetched from that dead knight in the River Green, yet John pinned the wing of a dragon piercing through rock hard scales. Neither Franklin, Quayfear, or John are magicians or sorcerers and the swords are ordinary, so it is as the Dresler said to John. The source of power was from the king himself.*

He sensed the sword beckoning him forward, but Daria's expression seemed to dare him to do it – that it was either her or this sword. Harbinger hesitated but then considered. Page had given his life to finding out what this mystery entailed, and the emissary saw fit to give him the responsibility of pursing it to its conclusion as his replacement. Page had placed his confidence in him. Harbinger knew what he had to do. He slowly removed the sword from its scabbard, took one last glance at Daria, walked over to the post aimed about four inches below the dwindling height of the pillar and swung and cut another chunk off of it.

He then turned to Daria, spoke solemnly, "Your turn."

Now it is him daring me! She slowly removed the sword and stared at it but did not move a muscle. It gleamed in the sunlight. She could not deny what she saw, but she could deny the source of its power. She slid the sword back into its sheath.

She looked at the three men, and spoke quietly but firmly, "I have a higher calling. This is why I cannot go with you. My reason for going to the Great City is not connected with that scroll. There is another reason I must go. I cannot expect you to understand. I wish you well in rescuing Lady Kettery and Ursula, but I cannot go with you." She stepped back and said goodbye, turned and left walking along the docks looking for passage to the Great City.

Harbinger noticed Quayfear look at him with his lips in the shape of a small circle, his eyes questioning, uncertain of how to respond to this woman's reaction, the one Harbinger was to marry. "It's all right," Harbinger said, calmly. "I must let her go."

20

Worlds Apart

Franklin, Luther, Brandish, and Brainwart had trudged along the River Green for six uneventful days. Tomorrow they would break away from the River Green and start up the narrow trail which wound its way to the Plains of Lanashear. The river had supplied them with plenty of fish to eat. Food would now be a concern.

The four men settled down for their last night along the river. The restful atmosphere was a blessing and a curse Franklin thought. As one basks in the glory of peace one must realize the enemy never sleeps. It was important that they not lose their edge. Anything could happen at any time in this place. Franklin lay on his back looking up into the darkness above. *What will greet us when we get to the plains - a great army led by this White King...or nothing*? Now that they were almost there, he began to have doubts.

The next morning they awoke to a cool but sunny day along the River Green. The early spring leaves swayed gently in a breeze that blew upstream. "We should be at the Plains of Lanashear by nightfall," Brainwart told them.

It was midday when the four men came to a fork in the road. "Which way?" Franklin asked Brainwart.

"To my recollection this was not here. There was one path from the river to the plains."

"I was wondering what would happen next? Now I know. One of these leads to the plains...the other leads to who knows where. Luther, you have a sword. Let Brandish use it for now, and you come with me."

And then turning to Brandish he said, "Take Brainwart down the path to the right. Luther and I will take the one to the left. Hopefully one of these paths just dies out or leads to some hermit's home. If it does not, we will meet back here by nightfall and then decide what course of action to take."

Luther and Franklin walked a half hour until they saw ahead of them something like a rectangle slab. "What is that?" Luther asked in wonder.

"It looks like a door," said Franklin, "but it is attached to nothing, standing upright across the trail."

"That is not normal. We need to go back!"

"Indeed, it is not normal," said a voice to their left. Luther and Franklin looked over. It was a man all dressed in olive green who spoke specifically to Luther as if Franklin was not there. "I was sent, Luther, to you to advise you to consider what the gods have offered."

"Who are you?" Luther asked.

"My name is Sourlip. I have been sent from the gods."

Luther was afraid. The man was tall, six foot six, his face boxy, his mouth wide and lips very thin. Luther determined if the gods were to send someone, this is what he would look like: angry, mean, and frightening. "You have been sent by the gods to me...why?"

"You have been chosen to receive mercy. Once in a great while the gods determine to show kindness to one who does not deserve kindness, for humans are irreparably displeasing to them." He gave a disgusting glance towards Franklin.

"What does this mercy bespeak?" Luther inquired.

"A mercy so great - that it even befuddles the gods why they should be so lenient to those who are so base, so frail...so weak. It is an opportunity that few will ever know. To receive this blessing you must pass through that door."

Franklin looked at him untrustingly. "What is on the other side?"

"I will show you," Sourlip said, though speaking directly to Luther and turned the knob and pushed open the door. Luther and Franklin saw nothing but forest to the left and right side of the door but through the opening they saw a village.

"It is a hamlet," said Franklin.

"It is Fartherwood!" Luther gasped, "But how...we are far from Fartherwood, nearly to the Plains of Lanashear. It is an illusion."

"No, Luther," said Sourlip in a deep corrective tone, "it is not an illusion. It is Fartherwood, but it is Fartherwood five weeks ago."

"What are you saying?"

"It is another world exactly as this one, though it is five weeks behind in time. Five weeks brings you back to the night you went to The Corner Tavern. You see Luther that world beyond the door is as real as this one but in a different time frame. You have been offered a rare gift. You may enter this other world and go back to the night you made that dreadful decision.

"You will enter that world with all your memories of what you did in this world intact. Therefore, you can undo that which under normal conditions could not be undone. You can return and choose not to join the others on that fateful morning, and you will end up in The Great City in a journeyman guild as originally planned. You have a chance to change a regret that has brought you here with no future. I can assure you that what lies ahead on the road you are on is far worse than that dragon.

"However, Luther, you have only five minutes to make up your mind. When the time is over or you willingly shut the door, it will disappear." Sourlip then turned and walked away, his clothing quickly blending into the greenery around them.

Luther looked at Franklin and stated enthusiastically, "I have been blessed by the gods!"

Franklin with a slight shake of his head responded in a wary and cautious tone, "Don't be so sure Luther. Not all gods bring us good tidings. Some are curses in disguise."

Luther snapped back, "You are jealous because you did not receive such an offer!"

"I did not receive the offer because I have no regrets of being here. Sourlip knows it is a waste of time to try and deceive me."

Luther took note of Franklin's demeanor and voice which remained calm and sagacious and it annoyed him. "I am here only because of this foolish decision I made that evening and all over that maiden Zelda! And now look at my life! How many people get a chance to do over a grave mistake, a misjudgment that sends their life reeling in the wrong direction?"

"No one gets such an opportunity - that is not the way life works. We have to learn from our mistakes and go on. We cannot go back." Franklin sighed in frustration seeing the blind enthusiasm Luther possessed, the willingness to barrel ahead into this unknown world, a world in which he didn't belong.

"No!" Luther demanded, now shaking his head in rebuttal. "There is nothing to learn from this mistake except that I have lost everything because of it."

"If you have lost everything, then it was everything you needed to lose in order to gain something more valuable."

"You heard Sourlip. What lies ahead is worse than facing the dragon."

"I will not give you false hope, Luther. The onward road is not going to be an easy one – I believe Sourlip has told the truth about that. But I think that you have an important destiny to fulfill here in this world, and the enemy wants you in another world where you cannot fulfill it."

Luther now poised relaxed for the first time and spoke with assurance of a future Sourlip spoke of. "I know if I go through that door I have a glorious future to fulfill in The Great City. If I stay here, I know where this road leads."

"You do not know where this road leads, Luther, nor do you know where the road in the other world leads. Do you think that you will never make another mistake, make a poor decision? There is no guarantee in that world you will end up in The Great

City…you might, you might not. You will not be able to undo future mistakes."

Luther was full of silent rage. He glanced back through the open door and saw fatty Farnbuckle waddling along, a young man known for his lethargic care-free attitude, and beyond him walked Zelda heading for The Corner Tavern to work there that fateful night that changed everything.

Luther suddenly realized there was one thing that was not going to be different in that world. Zelda would still hate him and show nothing but indifference towards him. She had never spoken kindly to him and barely acknowledged his existence. He realized how nice it was to be out of her purview, away from The Corner Tavern where she was unable to haunt him with her looks of disgust and dread every time he entered the establishment. Luther suddenly realized he did not want to see her, or hear her voice or have any contact with her ever again!

Franklin saw a sudden change in Luther's demeanor. He seemed angry and bitter but not at him. The wood worker with rancor grabbed the edge of the door and slammed it causing Franklin to step back in surprise.

At that moment the door disappeared. Franklin was perplexed, though pleased at Luther's decision. "You have chosen wisely," Franklin stated, not knowing what else to say or why the sudden reversal.

Luther stared at the empty trail ahead of them and turned towards Franklin with a look of horror. "What have I done?"

*

Brandish and Brainwart trudged on quietly with little to say to each other. After an hour of walking through the forest which seemed to be thinning out, Brainwart spoke, "Tell me Brandish who is this Franklin who seems to be in charge of this quest you are on. He hardly seems like leadership material – a scribe under a Baron is impressive among those in the city, but not out here in the wilderness where numerical acumen hardly comes close to what is needed.

"You, Brandish, one who has entered the testing grounds, one who has swung many a hammer, forged iron and bronze into all kinds of tools and weapons, muscular in tone and handsome in appearance with the advantage of youth resembles one chosen for a hardship such as this."

Brandish came to a halt and eyed the older man suspiciously, who appeared nothing like Sourlip the prophet's assistant, the one who visited him in his room in Wilderwood, the one who told him his destiny was to eventually replace Franklin as the sovereign leader of this journey when the opportunity presented itself.

Brainwart was squatty and tubular in appearance, yet his words sounded similar to Sourlip's. It was further evidence and confirmation that these two men – one a messenger of a prophet and the other a coward who ran from battle and hid deep in the woods, afraid to face anyone for decades because of his shame and disgrace have both arrived at the same conclusion – what is Franklin doing out here.

Brandish smiled to himself. His destiny was certain. At some point he would be in charge. Sourlip had stressed…be patient.

"The wood is thinning," Brainwart announced sharply, "we're nearing the plains. No need to go any farther. This is the way."

The two men started back to where the two paths met.

Brainwart and Brandish found Luther and Franklin waiting for them.

"This one leads to the plains," Brandish said. "Did yours lead anywhere particular?"

"Sort of," Luther said and then described the meeting with Sourlip and the opportunity he was offered.

Brandish was shocked that the prophet's assistant approached Luther. Then it dawned on him. Sourlip was attempting to save

Luther from coming to any harm from what lies ahead. *The time is nearly here. I must remain alert!*

*

By the time the four men arrived at the Plains of Lanashear the last glimmer of sun on the horizon emblazoned a swath of glowing amber just above the treeless landscape, and the tall dark grasses as far as they could see swayed gently in an evening breeze as if to give the weary travelers a warm welcome.

Yet Franklin did not experience any warm welcome but a bitter let down. There was no king, no army…no nothing. The scroll did not mention where to go once they had reached the plains, so his assumption was that someone would be waiting for them – that they would be expected…but they were alone.

"Look," Luther called out, "horses!"

Franklin turned hard and fast, and indeed, four mares stood off to their right tied to a tree on the edge of the plains. It wasn't much, but it was something. The men rushed over and opened the saddlebags. "This one has a note," Brainwart said. "Here, Franklin, you are the most educated among us - read."

"Do not eat this food until the morning. You will eat again when you reach the tabernacle where you will find Dresler waiting."

"I'm hungry now," Luther whined.

"We are all hungry," said Franklin, "but we have heeded the scroll so far, and it has not rung untrue, though for a brief moment I began to wonder. We must set aside our own feelings and designs, and do as instructed. We wait till morning." Franklin neatly folded the note and put it in his pocket.

Brandish looked across the open plains. "I don't think we will find any guilds or tradesmen out here Luther."

The woodworker shook his head in despair. "I should not have slammed that door. I should have gone through that door, got my commission to The Great City, wave them in Zelda's face and said goodbye to her forever!"

"Take heart Luther," Franklin encouraged, "I told you that your destiny is here in this world, yet I offered no proof. Your proof lies in that tabernacle – where we are headed tomorrow."

Luther was not impressed, but it was his only hope now.

21

Roads Diverge

Daria made her way along the tired looking shacks along the waterfront of Seven. She noticed a sailor sitting on a barrel lined up alongside five other barrels on a pier that jutted out to the sorriest looking boat she had ever seen.

The man called out to her, "You!" She turned, shot a glance at the man wearing drab olive green and looked at his pathetic Picard in the backdrop, a small sailing vessel used for short trips hugging the coastline. She resumed searching for something more reliable when he called out again, "Daria!"

She stopped abruptly and stared at the man who knew her name. He was not familiar. She approached him. The man was very tall and muscular, well adapted to a hard life at sea. It was not the sailor she questioned. It was the dilapidated condition of the boat. Could it even make it to the town of Six?

"Who are you? How do you know my name?" Daria asked in a confrontational tone.

"I am Sourlip, a servant of the prince of Genadar, a great spirit being who has taken an interest in you since you have left Fartherwood."

"I have not heard of this prince of Genadar. He means nothing to me?"

"He is an enemy of The White King – someone you have heard of, a king who has caused many a promising man to leave everything for the sake of his service, a service which only benefits this cruel king and leaves his proselytes abandoned and empty in the end. I have been told by my prince that you have weathered his deception. Our prince believes that you are in a position to aid him."

Daria looked on squinting from the glare off the water with caution and curiosity. "To what end?"

"Right now I can only ask you to please board my humble vessel."

Daria gave a disgusting frown. "Is that what you call it?" she stated mockingly. "I can think of a more descriptive term."

"You will find that it will do my lady."

"Are you heading To The Great City?"

"I am not permitted to divulge my destination unless you agree to join me, but I can tell you that I am sailing south."

"That is reason enough for me go with you."

Daria boarded the shanty boat, though hoping fair weather would follow; for surely it was questionable whether this shaky vessel could survive even the slightest squall.

*

Miles away across the Midland Sea in the forest of Genadar within the shadow of the Barrier Mountains, Marshstench, a fair maiden who had befriended Baron Durkel, stood by him beneath a tall tree. He had not mastered the language but could understand and speak well enough of weapons and strategies.

"Come," Durkel said to Marshstench, "let us review the workers' progress."

Marshstench smiled that big broad smile of hers and nodded. What seemed once strange and out of place to Durkel now seemed normal and even attractive. The two walked down a wide path. It soon opened up to a newly made clearing of trees that were recently cut milled and pegged together for catapults, siege ramps and towers; long ladders, a few ballistae, and a huge battering ram. Durkel was pleased with the swift progress of the laborers. Though their tools were crude and their construction designs simple and utilitarian, there was something soothing about the camaraderie of the large group.

Everyone worked together, no one working strictly on one thing as in the guilds. A woman making food for the men had stopped to help a pregnant mother walk over to a stump to rest her tired feet. A worker took time to speak to a young lad while pointing to the ropes which supported the battering ram as he explained how and where and why they were connected to the frame in such a way. He noticed three men working hard and yet taking a moment to laugh hardily at something someone said. The baron had to chuckle to himself. *And we call these people the barbarians.*

He had sent Letog, a member of the council, to the southern settlements to bring back the chieftains to speak to them of the prophecy from the prince about their conquest of the Midland Realm. He believed one look at their siege engines and the chieftains from the southern tribes would be eager to gather into one great force against the high walls of Vale.

Durkel had sent the chieftain's cousin Rakker to other tribes in the northern woods to invite them to view their war machines. Letog and Rakker had been gone about one week to their appointed destinations. He expected them both to return by the end of the month. Durkel glanced up at rain clouds above. He cursed realizing that this slowed down the work but then calmed himself. After all, they were spring showers, and it was the latter part of April, and they were much farther along than he would ever have imagined a couple of weeks ago.

No, things were going well. He was winning the hearts and minds of these people. They were forming a bond and relationship with him and not this prince. The chieftain and the council were cooperating, but the Baron had his sight on one particular tribal warrior who had befriended him. His name was Stumprot, whom he had recognized as the personal confidant to the one called Number Two – puppet to the prince of Genadar.

Inevitably the barbarians would be loyal to me, but eventually I will need my own number two, someone I can trust implicitly to share my own machinations of how this war will ultimately play out and who will actually control the Midland Realm. Stumprot is one of those spirit beings. If I can get him to leave the prince, then between the two of us, what could stop us – but I cannot do it without at least one of them. The question is what could entice Stumprot to leave the prince.

*

Number Two sat quietly alone in the bottom of the keep in Genadar, discouraged. He pounded his fist on the arms of his chair and then settled back and thought. *The episode with the dragon did not fare as predicted, and Sourlip mistakenly put Zelda in the picture, thinking it would lure Luther through that door on the trail but once again the unpredictability of these creatures has aided them well.*

However, much is in our favor. Daria has broken away from those with the special sword and is now in charge of her own fate. He chuckled...*which is no control at all. And those new converts John, Quayfear, and Harbinger are inexperienced with the special sword and are no match with what lies before them in the Pale Forest and Castle Calamitous. They will meet their end with the Harlequins of Glendyland.*

It is Franklin I am most worried about. He is on his way to the tabernacle. All our hope there lies with Brainwart and the people of the Plains. So much depends on them.

*

Dresler sat on the western bank of the River Green looking at Driftwood as it now inched its way imperceptibly out to sea, the roots below unable to hold the island back against the strong current. He then turned his gaze upriver where Merrill and those with him – Kia, Ewar, and Kingsley were on their way in pursuit of Harbinger, whom they believed killed the emissary.

Dresler heard the crunching of twigs and leaves from behind. He recognized that the pressure of these footsteps against the earth was not human. "Join me Fairhaven," he announced cheerfully without turning around.

The spirit being sat and spoke with a distraught resonance in his voice, "I am concerned, my Lord. Driscoll, the most obnoxious one of the group, was the only one who obeyed and remained in Driftwood. Lady Kettery and Ursula are going to Castle Calamitous. I can understand their concern for Beth, but to disobey the King seems contrary to any possible aid they can give Beth. And now Harbinger, John, and Quayfear, must come to their rescue...and who is going to rescue Daria from her ill-chosen destiny?"

"Not all things in this world are pleasant to watch or possible for you to understand, Fairhaven, but all are where they must be, and all things must run their course."

"I suppose their behavior is just the way of this world."

"Yes, Fairhaven, it is the way of this world, but the ways of this world will not determine the fate of this world."

Book 3: The Harlequins of Glendyland